Cowboy Come Home

Cowboy Come Home

A 79th Copper Mountain Rodeo Romance

Sinclair Jayne

TULE
PUBLISHING

Cowboy Come Home
Copyright© 2018 Sinclair Jayne
Tule Publishing First Printing, July 2018

The Tule Publishing Group, LLC

ALL RIGHTS RESERVED

First Publication by Tule Publishing Group 2018

No part of this book may be used or reproduced in any manner whatsoever without written permission except in the case of brief quotations embodied in critical articles and reviews.

This is a work of fiction. Names, characters, places, and incidents are products of the author's imagination or are used fictitiously. Any resemblance to actual events, locales, organizations, or persons, living or dead, is entirely coincidental.

Prologue

BOONE TELFORD WOKE before dawn like he always did. Automatically he sorted out the different birdcalls, but his attention was diverted by the warm, naked woman he was curled around. He could feel her long red-gold hair, silky across his face, shoulder and back, and he palmed one of her small, perfect breasts. Her lemon and honeysuckle scent made him feel drugged, and he breathed Piper in like an addict.

He pressed a line of kisses—soft, but with growing intent—down her spine.

She sighed happily, but couldn't roll over. He had her pinned down, her back to his front, his leg over hers.

"You awake?" he invited. She shouldn't be. He'd kept her up half the night. His hunger this summer, always a fierce ache that woke and rumbled several times a day around her, should have been assuaged by now. Four months on the road with the same woman.

Something he'd never done. Nor had it been the plan, although Boone had never been much of a planner. Roll-with-it Boone. His dad had teased him about his attitude when he'd been a tween and later a teen. He was twenty-five now, and nobody was laughing. His family wanted him home "where you belong," to help with the ranch and the planned expansion.

And he wanted…hell if he knew. This was supposed to be his make or break year. And he was killing it on the Montana pro rodeo circuit—better than he'd ever done. But there was Piper now to consider.

"Is your brachialis bothering you?" He heard the concern in her voice. How she came instantly awake. And his heart lurched.

Piper was in deep.

Hell, he was in deeper.

And even though inviting her on the rodeo tour with him this summer had been a lust-driven impulse he still couldn't quite explain, emotions were not supposed to be part of the equation.

But instead of starting to create the distance he was going to need between them, Boone rolled with the moment.

"I can't feel my brachialis, baby, but something else is causing me no end of problems."

"Really," Piper's voice was an inviting husk.

She reached behind her and wrapped her hand around his painfully hard erection. He went from playful and aroused to desperate even as he hissed in a breath.

"I need to be inside you," he said, voice raw, eyes stinging.

He rolled over so he was on top, bracing most of his weight with his hands and his arms as he caged her in.

Mine.

Possession flared as he saw the familiar contours of her heart-shaped face and unusual gray-green eyes that slanted up dramatically at the corners. She was a contradiction that fascinated him. Sweet but sexy. Exotic yet all-American. And always drop-dead beautiful even first thing in the morning tousled and loved.

She grinned at him, her eyebrows arched in challenge. She spread her legs and wrapped them around his taut, narrow hips.

"What are you waiting for, cowboy? Come home."

Chapter One

"MARIETTA MONTANA WAS founded in…"

Boone gripped the steering wheel of his Chevy Colorado truck. He knew when the town was founded. He knew the names of the original founding families and had attended school with their descendants. Hell, he even knew where the skeletons in many of those families were buried or stuffed in the closet. He was Marietta to his marrow.

And that was the problem.

He was being a jerk. Tuning Piper out. Something he'd never done. She read the Copper Mountain Rodeo website. He hadn't told her Marietta was his hometown. That he'd attended the Copper Mountain Rodeo since he was in diapers. That he'd won his first event—mutton busting—at age four there.

He hadn't once mentioned that they were heading down the mountain to his hometown.

But not to his home.

Not to his family.

Dick move and he knew it.

But he and Piper were never meant to go this far. Tour with him through the summer. Or less. That had always been the plan when he'd met her. Dillon two weeks ago had been the end of this road for them. Staring down the barrel of September. He thought at the end of August he'd put her on a plane to wherever she wanted to go. Only he hadn't. Hadn't said a word about goodbye. Instead he'd driven the horse trailer with the small living quarters from Dillon to compete in White Sulphur Springs.

He'd won a first in steer wrestling and bareback and third on the bull. And instead of celebrating at the bar and dancing, he'd taken Piper out to dinner and bought an obscenely expensive bottle of wine. Wine! A Bordeaux—whatever that was. And then he'd taken her to a spa so they could sit in the hot springs.

And he'd had a damn good time.

Not a cowboy in sight.

He hadn't mentioned the airport.

Or how he should be ending it that night.

Or definitely this morning.

Or that the next stop on the Montana pro rodeo circuit was his hometown. And that his father was one of the rodeo planners. And his family would all be there expecting him to come home—stay at the ranch. Sit with them during all the social events like the picnic, steak dinner, pancake breakfast. Work the ranch the week after before heading to Great Falls.

And all that was now shot to hell. He wiped his forehead

with the back of his hand.

His family didn't know about Piper. She didn't know about them.

And he had no idea how he could keep it that way.

He glanced over. She was wearing a cute racer-back sporty sundress and one of his shirts tied around her slim waist for warmth. Her hair was in a messy knot on top of her head that he could barely resist pulling out. She sat cross-legged and was scrolling through the website like she did for every rodeo—fully immersed in the experience.

In two miles, she'd lose cell service.

He should tell her now about Marietta. His family.

But his tongue stuck to the roof of his mouth. His throat dried. He felt like someone he didn't know.

And he definitely didn't like.

Boone scowled at the twisting steep grade ahead.

He'd met Piper in May. In California at the beach. A cliché and he damn well knew it.

Cowboy sees the ocean for the first time and a girl with long, red-blonde hair and longer legs, wearing one of those lacy bikinis. Cowboy loses his mind. Boone mocked himself. He was not admitting to losing his heart but he sure as hell felt hollow when he thought of cutting her loose.

Piper had tossed him on his dumb ass harder than any prime, pissed-off thrashing bull or bronc.

Head over heels as the country singers crooned.

Piper was way out of his league. Boone had known it

then, and he knew it now. Didn't make a lick of difference. He rode bareback broncs and bulls and wrestled steers to the ground for fun, prize money and to prove a point. He'd never backed down from a challenge. And Piper had seemed like the biggest one of his life. So he'd tried his chances.

"Travel with me for a bit on the rodeo tour this summer," he'd impulsively asked after they'd spent an afternoon and evening together. "You can see Montana."

Piper had two college degrees and had lived all over the world. She'd danced professionally. He'd expected her to laugh at him. Instead he'd watched her get her certificate in massage therapy in a small Saturday afternoon ceremony in a teacher's home garden, and then she'd packed up a small leather backpack and a duffel bag of her clothes and climbed in his truck.

And here they were. September.

And neither he nor Piper had said anything about ending it.

But he had to. There was no place for them to go.

He'd just turned twenty-five.

At his age his dad had been a rodeo god. Two-time bull-riding champ and four-time bareback. He'd had a case of buckles, a shelf full of trophies and enough prize money to rescue his family's ranch from bankruptcy. Hell, at twenty-five his father had met one of Montana's most beautiful and accomplished rodeo queens and married her three months later. Within a year they had their first baby.

"I saw her ride, and when she got off the horse and smiled at me, I was done. End of the line. Thought she wouldn't give me a chance but I was gonna do my best to ride to the end of the bell." Boone had heard his dad tell that story enough and the parallels were not lost on him although Piper had been on a paddleboard, something he hadn't even known existed until he saw her on one.

But that was the end of the similarities with his dad. Boone had buckles. He had wins. But nothing like his dad. He had money saved, but wasn't sure it was enough for the down payment to buy the small spread that was coming up for auction later this year. He'd coveted that small piece of land partially bordering his family's ranch since his teens.

Yeah, Boone could make his life on his family's ranch. It was what his mom and dad wanted. But Boone wanted to be his own man. Make his own way.

And getting turned inside out by a woman and spending time with her, instead of honing his skills, wasn't going to help him make his mark.

He slowed the truck's speed further as he headed down the mountain pass into Paradise Valley. For once he wasn't eager to see Marietta nestled in the shadow of Copper Mountain, wasn't anticipating one of his mom's home-cooked meals or riding the land with his dad and checking out the new stud bull he'd purchased—the one that had almost killed his dad last February.

"The town has a saloon. A real saloon." Piper's melodic

tone rose in awe and her gray-green eyes glowed. "Can you imagine? It's called Grey's Saloon. It's still open and it's run by the descendants of Ephraim Grey."

Damn, the girl loved history. And she loved reading. She often read while he drove the truck—fiction, politics, biographies, articles. The world came alive in Piper's dulcet tones, and her voice had a husk to it that always turned him on, but also made him feel protective.

"Grey's Saloon was the first building in Marietta, and there was a balcony where the ladies of the brothel used to stand and catcall down to potential customers. I wonder if it's still there."

It was.

Dammit. Guilt made him want to crawl out of his skin.

"I hope we have time to go there, Boone."

"We'll make time," he said, loving the way the mid-morning light played on her hair—turned that thick red-gold mass into liquid fire.

"Grey's has dancing. And with the rodeo in town, you know a lot of cowboys will be hitting the dance floor."

"I've been known to two-step a time or two."

Her smile held the promise of a sunrise. Her finger trailed along his thigh, and her hand rested there. A brand. Hers. He couldn't lie to himself about that. His response was fierce. Painful. Not just his cock—he could deal with that—but everything inside him hurt as well. Felt broke, but when she touched him, he felt whole again.

Dumb.

He'd never been known to analyze anything except an engine or an animal. Why was he getting so…he didn't even know what the word was, and he didn't want to find out.

"Piper." He couldn't wrestle the urgency out of his voice.

She turned fully toward him. And he had trouble swallowing. Heck, he could hardly remember his own damn name. Her creamy skin always begged for his hands, or his mouth, and he had a hard time resisting her now even as they barreled down the mountain. She leaned toward him, his shirt slipping off her shoulders, leaving them bare and kissable. Available. She was like that. Warm. Sensual, curling up into him like a cat. She was so tactile. Loving. And he'd come to crave the contact. She brought him a peace he'd never known could exist.

And feeling calm and content at twenty-five when he hadn't made his mark would spell disaster.

"You're tense, Boone." Her keen eyes assessed him, and he struggled to not squirm because Piper read him as well as she did all the books she downloaded on her Kindle. "Are you in pain? We have time. I could work on your shoulder and arm tendons and ligaments—loosen them up." Her words were innocent. Her tone was tender with a hint of professionalism that should not have turned him on. He wasn't an invalid. He was often in pain and ignored it, but Piper made him long to be soothed.

Piper's full lips pouted a little as she visually assessed

him. Boone shifted. Damn, if she didn't stop looking at him like that, he was going to have to pull over to adjust himself. Or let her do it for him. That would solve the problem that had started eating away at him since Dillon if he drove off the road killing them both.

"You were reading to me about Marietta," he said a little desperately.

Piper leaned closer. He felt the brush of her lips along his exposed collarbone and then her tongue swirled at the base of his Adam's apple. Her hair was like silk against his neck and caught a little in the stubble along his jaw, even though he'd shaved this morning. Her small breasts, sweetly contained in a stretchy peach bandeau bra that he'd already pulled off with his teeth this morning when she'd been trying to get dressed, brushed his arm.

Fuck it.

He needed to pull over. He'd driven Highway 89 hundreds of times, but his mind came up blank about turnouts.

Piper laughed.

"The name Copper Mountain Rodeo comes from Marietta's brief copper mining boom in the late eighteen eighties."

Her voice was magic—drawing him in and jacking him up even as dread curled in the pit of his stomach. His phone tucked uncomfortably in his back pocket so Piper wouldn't see it as it continued to blow up for the last fifty miles—voice messages and texts from his friends and family. Hell, even his half-brother, Witt, the orthopedic surgeon, had texted—joking that he hoped he saw him vertical, not horizontal in his OR. Not funny. But Witt wasn't funny.

Boone had made the mistake of listening to a few voice messages when they'd stopped at a café and Piper had stood in line for a chai. He had over a dozen messages from family and friends—invitations for beer, dinner, game of pool, and his family was expecting him at the ranch. His room was ready. It was always ready.

He'd nearly lost the tofu and veggie breakfast burrito—wrapped in a damn almond flour tortilla—Piper had cooked for him earlier that morning because she was worried about his cholesterol. He rolled his eyes at himself for being so caught up in her that he'd actually eaten it. Not to mention enjoyed it. But WTF! He was just twenty-five. In his prime. He was a cowboy. Ranch all the way. He couldn't eat vegan. He'd get mocked off the circuit. Kicked out of town. His dad raised cattle for fuck's sake.

This was goddamn Montana.

And if he brought Piper home…his family would have a barn wedding planned and start construction converting one of the riverside cabins by the end of the weekend. He'd be off the circuit and working the ranch like he'd done his entire life.

He'd forever be Boone Telford, Taryn Telford's youngest son. That clever surgeon Witt's cowboy youngest brother. The war hero special ops soldier Rohan's little brother. The rising country and pop singer Riley's big brother.

He'd be tied to them. No accomplishments of his own.

He had to cut bait. It wasn't fair to Piper. She screamed perfect and permanent down to the marrow of his bones.

But he couldn't be the man to give her the permanent home and family she craved.

Not yet.

But Piper was now.

Way too fucking soon.

And he had to man up or else he'd make them both miserable.

Chapter Two

"OH, THIS SHOULD be the 80th Copper Mountain Rodeo, but the grandstand burned down last year in August. Arson, but no one was charged. Who would do that? Crazy. Were you signed up for that rodeo, Boone?"

He sucked in a breath. He had to tell her. He'd been raised to do the right thing. Always.

God, her eyes, that gray green, the slightly almond shape and the long curved sweep of lashes always sucked him in. Her unusual heart-shaped face where every expression chased across it, so easy to read. He was drowning. He barely managed to tear his eyes away and back to the road. Hell, he was coming up on the spot Harry Monroe had been killed. Harry had been two years ahead of him at school. Nicest kid ever.

Same thing everyone says about me.

Only now he was being a grade A asshole.

"Haven't missed it in eight years."

Make that twenty-five, but seven competing. And who's counting?

He also hadn't made all-around cowboy. Or placed higher than second professionally on any event in his hometown. Last year he hadn't even made it to the short round, he'd been so tired and beat up. Sure. He was good. Better than good. Sometimes great. But not legendary.

Not Taryn Telford. His father.

"Then you must know the town." Her lips curved in that smile that always broke his heart a little, made him want to be a better man. "It says here…"

Wait for it.

She'd lose cell service as soon as they swung around the next curve. And he wouldn't have to hear about all the joys of Marietta for another ten miles.

Piper made an exasperated sound, placed her cell phone in the cup holder and kicked up her bare feet onto his dash. Electric-blue polish on her toes. She had beautiful feet. She disagreed. She'd been a dancer so she had a lot of callouses. But he loved how they fit in his hands. How her eyes would roll back and she'd gasp and moan and whisper his name when he would massage her feet with warm oil. Before he moved north on her body.

Ironic as hell since she was the professional.

"It's the twenty-first century," she griped. "Why am I losing cell service twenty or so miles out of a town? On a highway? This is America! What happened to we're number one and make it great again?"

He laughed at her outrage.

"In London you can talk on the tube and that's deep underground."

"Not a lot of rodeos in London," he said without thinking. Could he sound like more of a hick? Piper had traveled the world.

She grinned. "Those London girls don't know what they're missing."

He liked how she always had a comeback. How conversation was so easy with her. She asked him a lot of questions because she was interested. Yet, sometimes, she could be so still and lay outside his trailer in the summer grass while he felt each breath she took and she'd stare at the spangled sky without a word.

And her citrus and honeysuckle scent always made him hungry.

"Boone! Look! Stop. Pull over!"

He knew without asking what had caught her attention. Piper loved the scenery when they traveled as much as he did. She never complained when they made a photo op stop.

"Oh my God," she breathed. "That is so beautiful."

He was already signaling, pulling over. There was a small turnout because it was a well-remarked view point—a beautiful alpine lake nestled in the Gallatin Mountains. He stopped the truck and checked his mirrors to ensure the trailer was completely off the road. Usually he'd check on his horse, but they hadn't been driving long, and they were close to the rodeo grounds. It wasn't even noon on Thursday.

They had plenty of time.

Usually he rushed this part of the trip home, eager to see his family, take some of the burden off his father, catch up with friends, but today, because he was *not* manning up, he was happy to stop.

Piper spilled out of the truck, a flash of long, toned legs on the side of the road.

"Ouch!" She dashed across the asphalt toward the grass for a better view.

"Baby—" he caught her easily and swung her into his arms "—you're barefoot," he said, pointing out the obvious.

She was often barefoot. It made him crazy and turned him on at the same time. She sighed and threaded her fingers through the back of his hair—which he was going to have to chop off soon. His mom and sister would give him grief. He was practically sporting a mane, but when he'd met Piper, he'd been long overdue for a haircut and Piper had been very physically and verbally demonstrative over his thick, shaggy hair.

Damn, one more sign he was whipped.

He put her down, wrapped his arms around her, and rested his chin on the top of her silky head. She crept back so that the soles of her feet rested on his cowboy boots. He didn't try to hide his smile.

"I bought you boots," he reminded her.

"Two pairs."

"Gonna glue 'em on, baby. Can't have my girl at the rodeo barefoot."

Her body relaxed into his, and for the first time this morning, he felt settled. Everything right.

"It's called Miracle Lake," he said, letting the strands of her fiery hair catch in his lips. God, sometimes he was worried he would hurt her, hold her so tight she'd bruise.

"Do you know what the miracle was?"

That was Piper, always wanting to learn.

"There mighta been a few over the years. Stories change depending on who's telling. Long while back a boy fell through the ice. Was pulled out. Dead. Not breathing. No pulse."

Piper's breath hitched. He loved that too. Her sensitivity.

And he was going to hurt her. He knew he would.

He closed his eyes tightly and buried his face in her hair. Slipped the elastic band from her messy bun so the red-gold mass just blew around them in the breeze racing down from the higher elevations into Paradise Valley.

"So the rescuers wrapped him up, breathed for him. Maybe did CPR and then he opened his eyes. He'd been dead a while. But was brought back to life. No permanent damage."

"Boone." She pressed her hands over his, and he felt the tremble to his bones. "Losing a child. It's the worst pain of all."

She was so stiff and quiet. He paused. Curious. The pain in her voice. He'd never heard anything like it before from her. Piper was always easy, soothing him. Lifting him up when he crashed.

"Piper?" he questioned, and without meaning to he slipped his hands lower, covered her abdomen, wondered if there was something in her past she hadn't shared. "The boy didn't die," he assured her after a beat of silence. "He was fine. It's a local legend. He grew up. Had a family. All the normal things."

"Normal," he thought she whispered, but the breeze stole her words. "Any other miracles this lake has produced?" She turned in his arms and pressed a kiss where his shirt parted at his throat, a little above his heart. It was as high as she could reach unless he helped her. Boone usually preferred taller girls he didn't have to stoop to kiss, but Piper had snuck in under his guard and settled in.

"Well, maybe not everyone would think this was a miracle, but during the winter lots of folks go ice skating on the lake, and a couple of Christmases ago, a man, Laird Wilder arrived in Marietta with some hard questions about his life and family he was searching for. He lit a bunch of candles on the ice and went skating in the dead of night. And as he prayed for answers, he met a local woman, who was a bit of a town bad girl, but a hella barrel racer, Tucker McTavish.

"Anyway, she too was aiming to change her life. She wanted absolution for a lotta things to hear her tell it, but mainly from her sister who was marrying a cowboy Tucker had once fancied, and well, she and Laird met that night, fell in love and then he found the answers he was seeking. Turned out he too was born local, a twin, but he and his brother were adopted out separately so he'd never met his birth mother or his twin, and by Christmas a month after he made his prayer, he'd found his family and the love of a good woman. They still live here in Marietta. Married. Happy."

And were poised to do business with his father. Business that his father really wanted him to move home and join as a full-time partner.

Piper turned her face up. Her eyes were shiny with tears, her expression sober.

"Love is a miracle," she stated.

He found it hard to breathe. His skin prickled, and he felt like he was burning up inside. He hadn't used that word with her, but a lot of unnamed feelings beat around his head like caged birds. And he had to keep that door locked up tight.

"It is," he said, his voice tight.

Piper searched his face, but Boone looked back out toward the view.

"That's a beautiful local story," Piper said quietly. "How'd you hear it?"

"Like I said, Tucker was a barrel racer."

Different circuit than him. And she'd been the revered beautiful high school bad girl barely graduating senior to his middle school attempts at swagger.

"Finding your family and your forever home would be a

miracle," Piper snuggled closer, her lips doing something to his skin that felt like she was lighting matches.

Hard to argue with that.

"Can you take me to Miracle Lake, Boone? Do we have time? Can we get there from here?"

There were two ways to take that question. Literal or symbolic he supposed.

The first he could manage. The second? Boone didn't know how to be that man. If he'd met Piper a few years from now, he'd want to be. But wanting got you nothing. Doing mattered.

He took her hand and flipped it over, palm up. Being with Piper was strange. In some ways it was a little like getting on that bucking bronc or bull. Holding on. Euphoric. Alive. All cylinders firing and then a second before the bell, the monster ducks his head or drops a shoulder, or kicks left when you thought right, but that stunt and the laws of physics just kick your blissed-out state of mind to the fence and your hurtled body just rag dolls right along with it.

He and Piper were about to get tossed off.

Hard.

"Yeah, baby. I'll take you."

THE WATER WAS cold. Colder than she'd anticipated. Piper had imagined…what, stripping off her clothes and running naked across the gravelly sand and splashing into the dark blue water? Maybe in a book. But here there was a family picnicking out of earshot but definitely within view. And a couple of fishermen in boats on the lake.

So Piper had changed into her bikini and was wading cautiously into the water instead of running and jumping, while Boone leaned against a picnic table, arms crossed, eyes intent on her, and looking hot and perfect and… She sighed. Hers. She wanted him to be hers. Hers in a way no one had ever been before, and so many times during the day and especially at night she felt like he was. Everything she'd ever dreamed of. Strong and kind and caring and fun and so into her body that she kept looking into the mirror trying to figure out what the big deal was. But then she'd catch a look or…or a shadow or a drop in Boone's energy like he was suddenly absent and dread would sweep through her.

"Don't be stupid. You'll ruin everything," she whispered to herself.

Boone was magic. And for once she didn't want to overanalyze everything and make the safe decision—the so-called right decision. She wanted to go with her heart.

She'd never had anything close to what she had with Boone. Not in high school—hard to when she was moving every year and sometimes more. And not in college as she'd ground through her dance and kinesiology majors in less than four years. Definitely not in the dance company with the hours of rehearsal followed by performances and then moving to another city, another rehearsal space and theater, every day or so.

And then she'd left the dance world behind. She'd wanted a place to call home. Friends. Family. So she'd gotten certified in massage and the day before she walked in the ceremony she'd gone to Newport Bay to celebrate by herself like she'd done all her life and then like magic, Boone had appeared.

He'd walked toward her with a rolling, fluid stride that stole her breath and exploded her mind.

His eyes had never left hers, and the determination in his jaw had filled her with awe. Excitement. A sense of destiny that she still felt. And when he'd shrugged out of his shirt she'd been unable to stop her jaw from dropping.

Boone had definitely noticed. Even his eyes had laughed.

"Like what you see?" he'd teased before he'd even introduced himself. And his playfulness and audacity had crushed her protective wall. "Because I do, and I was thinking about trying one of those things." His blue gaze had briefly skimmed the paddleboard and then returned, lighting her up in a way she'd never experienced and made her feel dizzy. "If you're willing to share."

And then he'd smiled at her.

Bright as the sun.

Eyes blue as the sky. Smile as wide as the Milky Way and dimples like craters on the moon. He'd looked at her like she was special. Piper felt special with Boone. And she'd been willing to share far more than the paddleboard.

"You swimming or trying to catch fish by letting them nibble on your toes?" Boone called out amused, tugging her back to the present. "Because toe nibbling is my job."

"It's cold," she said. "I thought the Pacific was chilly but this is bone-cracking icy."

"Girl, this is Montana. Glacier fed. Not water rolling in from the white and black sand beaches of Hawaii." He let his voice slide all country and that never failed to soak her panties.

"That's right," she said letting her voice turn to smoke. "You're a cowboy."

"Damn straight. To my soul. One hundred percent Montana cowboy. The kind your momma and daddy warned you about," he teased, not moving from his sexy slouch against the picnic table.

Her mother hadn't stuck around long enough to warn her about anything.

God. He was such a man. Like she'd always dreamed of. She was crazy about him, and her father would stroke out to know that with all of her education and 'worldly exposure to politics and culture,' she had fallen hard and irrevocably for a cowboy.

Not that she'd tell him. Or that he'd ask. If she did go for a visit, which she likely wouldn't, she'd probably only get five minutes with him at his office on whatever base he was currently stationed before he'd call some suck-up to take her somewhere he wasn't—a museum, symphony, dinner.

"But not anymore," she said softly. She'd made a promise to herself. A vow. And she would keep it.

"Baby, it's so cute when you talk to yourself."

She nearly jumped to see Boone striding through the water toward her. Hat off. Shirt off. Jeans off. Boots off. Just the black boxers that hugged his butt, thighs and the thing she was obsessed with. Who knew with her few tepid, fumbling sexual forays in college that had left her embarrassed and even lonelier, that she would become so sexually driven?

"Clearly the water's not that cold." His voice slid through her ears and through her blood, heating her. He looked down and she could see how hard he was. The tip of his cock poked through his waistband.

"Boone." Excitement slithered through her, and her heart kicked up like she was on her morning run. "There's a family at the north end of the lake. And fishermen on the opposite shore."

He laughed. "Look at you with the compliments. Like they can see me. You talk like that to a cowboy, girl, you're gonna need to do something about it."

His eyes were nearly navy with desire, and the heat he threw off puddled her core.

Her breathing fractured. She stared at him, ignoring the view of the lake, the trees, the huge mountain glowering at them. The world, no, the universe narrowed down to Boone. His broad shoulders. The defined muscles of his pecs, and the corded muscles of his shoulders and arms and his abs that could never be sculpted in a gym.

And she knew he had strength. And stamina. He proved it to her every night. She still couldn't believe he was real. That he was hers.

"I can't breathe," she whispered, so caught in his spell that she'd given up even pretending he didn't completely undo her every time.

"You hot for me baby? Wet?"

"Standing in water," she said.

"My girl's funny. You know what I meant. Do I need to check for myself?"

She nodded. He reached for her and she melted. She could feel him hard against her abdomen. A molten steel spike that could make her scream and beg and forget her own name. His large, calloused hand slipped between their bodies and dipped into her bikini. One finger curled deep inside her.

"Boone," her legs noodled. "We're sort of in public."

"Makes it more exciting doesn't it?" He withdrew his finger and licked it, his eyes on her. He tilted his head as if thinking, and Piper thought she'd die from excitement. "Not wet enough," he concluded.

Then he lifted her and launched her into the air. Piper yelped and splashed into the icy water and came up spluttering. Boone was already flat-out swimming toward her like a shark. His gaze intent. Excitement flared and she turned and began to freestyle across the lake. Her laugh broke free and rolled out across the water. She loved to swim, and she loved to play with Boone more than anything.

"Catch me if you can, cowboy."

Chapter Three

"Boone! Good to see you."

"Boone. You still gluttoning for punishment on the back of any beast that will give you a chance?"

"Boone…could you take a look at…?"

Piper liked that Boone was popular. Usually they rolled into the rodeos the afternoon or the night before. After four months, she too knew many of the cowboys on the tour, but it seemed there was always someone new in each town, and then others leaving—injuries, broke or life's demands. Still Boone knew almost everyone. And he'd always slip his strong arm around her waist, introduce her, have a funny story about everyone. And he'd get roped into helping with a cowboy's rig or his trailer or equipment. And he never said no.

Once he got his horse settled, Boone always helped her set up her small tent and massage equipment. Now with her earnings she'd purchased a commercial-grade Pilates reformer to provide deep stretches for her clients, which had initially garnered a lot of snickers and one-liners about bondage and S & M, but once she'd stretched out a few cowboys before their events, her bookings had grown and the attitude was more grateful and blissed out instead of overt sexual snark. Although she still got that, just a little more subtly.

And no one had failed to note that Boone's ranking had gone up steadily since May.

Buying the portable massage equipment had been Boone's idea.

"Can't think of a cowboy who's going to say no to a beautiful woman laying hands on him." Boone had laughed, then paused. "They'll have clothes on, right?"

"Did you last night?" she'd teased, remembering the massage she'd treated him to as part of her "graduation requirements skills demonstration."

"Damn." Boone had shaken his head in mock disapproval. "Think I'll need to put a leash on you."

Piper dragged her attention back to the present. She had work to do and dreaming about Boone wasn't going to get it done. She rinsed off in the small shower in their trailer and changed into yoga capris and a tank so she could get her booth set up. She spotted Boone in the center of a group of men on the other side of the temporary field parking lot. They were deep in conversation, and one man with dark hair was pointing toward the arena.

Piper started toward them. Like always, Boone seemed to have a radar around her and he looked up. A frown chased across his face before his features settled into more neutral territory. His eyes shuttered and Piper's heart stuttered.

He'd never looked at her like that. Ever. He held up his hands, all fingers spread, and then jerked his head toward the trailer.

He'd help her set up her traveling masseuse equipment in ten. Got it. Piper tried to push down the warning that shivered down her spine, and smiled back. Her sunny smile that she used when she didn't always feel like smiling but she didn't want anyone to know. When she needed to feel brave and wanted.

Boone walked off with purpose. His strong, long legs ate up the ground as he headed off toward the outbuildings where the stock would be held. Several of the men followed him. She could also see the top of the grandstand peeking through a break in the buildings. Not too many cowboys had arrived yet. Boone had already leveled his small trailer and detached his truck and settled his horse, Sundance, in a stall.

Piper raised the awning and rolled out a western motif carpet and added the two fold-out chairs and a small table. She warmed up the Keurig machine, knowing Boone would soon want coffee, and she could make herself a quick chai.

The sun gleamed overhead in a brilliant blue sky. Piper looked longingly toward the end of the field and a stand of trees. It looked so pretty and inviting. From the map she thought the downtown was in that direction, and she thought she could just catch a glimpse of the top of a domed building. Piper was tempted to go exploring, but she knew she should get her tent set up—not always expect Boone to help her. Even though he still loped around the front of his truck to open her door every time.

Piper worried her top lip between her teeth. Maybe Boone felt she was taking him for granted. She needed to be independent. Not a burden. He should be able to go off with his friends, not feel like he had to entertain her. Guys hated that, didn't they? Her father had never wanted her around. And Piper had never had a boyfriend before Boone.

Tent. Then the massage table and chair. And the sign that she'd designed. She wasn't going to just play the girlfriend following Boone around weekend after weekend. Or worse, she felt herself flush, a buckle bunny.

She unlocked and then popped off the lid of the truck's bed and slid it off the back.

"Hey." A huge man accompanied by a young boy and a large white dog strode up to the truck. "Let me help you with that."

"Oh, I'm fine," Piper said, a little intimidated by the sheer size and energy of the man.

"I'm helping my sister-in-law, Sky, near the entrance in a few, but I got time to get…is this a tent?…set up. Where do you want it?"

"Thank you, but really I don't want to trouble you."

"No trouble." He easily lifted the truck bed lid over his head, slid it under the trailer and with one hand lifted out the massage table. He rested it against a tire and then grabbed the chair.

Sheesh. Her equipment was mobile, but not toy size or weightless.

"Okay, then, Superman."

"No, Colt Ewing Wilder."

Piper scrunched her eyes shut. She'd said that aloud.

"Piper Wiley," she said, smiling at the little boy. So much easier than facing down her embarrassment with his father.

The boy looked to be eight or nine. He grinned at her and shook her hand.

"I'm Parker Wilder. We're like name twins," he said. "With names this close." He held his palms together nearly touching. "We could be family."

Piper felt like her chest was pierced with an icicle. A family. The thing she'd never really felt she had.

"That's my dad. Tall, huh? My mom's tall too. She's studying to be a vet. This is our dog, Dude. I named him. Why are you bringing a table and a chair to the rodeo? The grandstand is rebuilt so there's lots of seats. There was a fire. A big one." He made an explosion sound.

Piper laughed. She couldn't help it.

"I'm a masseuse," she said.

"A what?" Parker stared. "Never seen that event."

"It's a profession." She bit back a smile.

"So do you want the tent to be in the back where the

cowboys limber up?" Colt asked. "Or is it for the public?"

"I've…um…been…working with the cowboys before and after they ride when they feel they need it."

Colt nodded and headed off like he knew where he was going, which was good because she had no idea. "Parker, carry the tent poles," he called out.

Parker scrambled into the truck and started grabbing the blue vinyl fabric that was rolled around the tent poles. Holding it, Parker jumped down to the ground.

"Can you grab the hammer and ropes?" Parker asked as he ran after his dad.

Piper swallowed her burst of independence, picked up the hammer, supporting cables and her sign. Before she followed the father and son, she pulled out a cooler that had some sparkling waters and juices as well as a container of oatmeal and dried fruit cookies she'd made last night. If the people of Marietta were going to be hospitable, who was she to hold back? She'd been looking for a small town to settle in. She shouldn't waste this opportunity to learn more about this one. She liked the beauty of Montana. And four seasons would be interesting.

Not that Boone had asked her to stay once the tour was over. But he hadn't talked about her leaving either.

Piper squared her shoulders and tried to ignore the instinctive protest at the thought of parting ways with Boone. He'd promised the summer. Not forever. Their affair was supposed to be fun, an impulse, a chance to see the Big Sky

Country and a few of the surrounding ones, and why not? She was young and free and while she'd seen so much of the world, she'd seen none of the American west. She'd known nothing of cowboys or rodeos.

Or love.

But Piper had faced the truth long before she and Boone had watched Fourth of July fireworks sprawled on the grass of a small-town park. She was deeply in love with Boone Telford. She couldn't imagine a day spent without him.

And his distraction and coolness today were making her think she might have to start.

By the time she'd found Colt and Parker, her tent poles had been pounded into the ground by a mallet that was looped through Colt's pants. Parker had rolled out the thick vinyl material of the tent, and she and Colt spread it out and looped the material through the support poles and tied it off.

"Pretty slick." Colt felt the fabric. He carried in her table and chair. "That had to set you back some."

It had set Boone back. Piper felt herself flush. Boone had wanted her protected from the elements, especially the sun.

"I have a carpet I put in here so I'll set the table and chair up tomorrow," she said feeling a little shy. She pulled out a container of cookies and offered them to Colt and Parker. Colt took one. Parker took two with an impish grin, holding one in each fist.

"We can carry the carpet in," Parker said. "I'm getting muscles like my dad." He flexed.

She avoided looking at Colt and his massive chest and arms. He could probably carry the rug she'd bought in Turkey with one curled finger.

"Let's do it, P. You figure out how to unfold the chair and then we'll meet Aunt Sky."

"Really, I can…" Piper trailed off as the little boy began to eye the clasps and hinges on the chair with interest. It had taken Piper twenty minutes to set up the chair the first time and none of those minutes had involved success. Boone had figured it out in two minutes. It took Parker five. So much for her blaze of independent spirit.

Five minutes later her traveling masseuse business was good to go without her breaking a sweat and Colt and Parker had each grabbed another cookie and ducked out of her tent.

"Welcome to Marietta," Colt said.

BOONE WOUND QUICKLY around the outbuildings. He'd been gone longer than he'd anticipated. Piper hadn't texted. She rarely did. She gave him a lot of independence. Always smiling, letting him go off with the other cowboys to drink after a win or a loss if he wanted. Over the past four months, he hadn't wanted. But saying no to a hometown crowd was not as easy. And dodging his dad's invitation to dinner had been like a damn UN meeting.

"Let's hit Grey's," his dad had urged. "Everyone's going to be there. The town's been thirsting for the rodeo. You can help me write my speech for tomorrow. Hate public speeches, but they still keep dragging me out of mothballs and kicking me up the steps to one stage or another. This year I'm in the damn parade. A float. Not even a horse."

Boone had looked at his father. Mothballs his ass. His dad's hair was still jet black—barely any threads of silver, and it remained thick and shiny. He was still crazy fit—long days at the ranch will do that, and from what Boone had experienced all his life, his dad loved his wife, kids, ranch, animals and always gave back to the community.

"I'll go," Boone had promised rashly. "But I got a couple of things to do first. I'll be there in thirty."

He'd be late to meet his dad, his friends. He was already late to help Piper. This was stupid. Impossible. But he knew the minute he told her he was Marietta born and bred, she'd wonder why he hadn't said anything. And then she'd ask about his family. And why he'd never gone home for a visit in four months—something his family had not overlooked, and were alternately curious, irritated and hurt about.

And of course they'd love Piper. She and Riley would hit it off. And his mom would give him that smile. And his dad would slap his back. Start pushing more of his plans for the ranch expansion with the Wilders and bull breeding. And a rodeo school.

He'd walk his dad's path.

Not his own.

Not that he knew what it was.

Yet.

He did know he didn't want to spend his life only as Taryn Telford's son and Witt and Rohan's younger brother. His country-rock singing sister's big brother. He needed his own string of accomplishments before he became someone's husband and father. A man he'd be proud of.

"Hey, baby," he called out as he came up to his truck. Piper was stretched out, shins and feet on the brown, cream, black and green swirled carpet and then she arched back around so that her hands gripped her feet and her forearms and elbows also rested on the carpet. Her thick ponytail curled on the soles of her feet. She wore yoga capris and a racer-back tank. And no bra.

Boone could barely swallow. What the hell had he needed to do that was more important than being with Piper? From the yoga cards she leafed through each day hoping to draw him into more poses than the basics, he thought this pose was called kapotasana.

He adjusted himself and tried to drag his mind out of the gutter, but dang this girl made it hard to elevate his thoughts above his buckle most days.

"Sorry I'm late."

She uncurled from the pose and rolled onto her stomach, feet over her head and touching the ground.

Jesus, was she trying to kill him?

"You could join me, cowboy." Piper smiled at him, her eyes soft.

His stomach flipped, but he tried to keep his voice light. The moment she'd looked at him, four months ago, the attraction had been a punch to the gut. He'd felt almost desperate to be with her. He'd felt nothing like that before. Time should have dimmed the pull. Instead it just cranked it higher.

He was going to blow this. Hurt her. Or ruin his future and make them both unhappy.

"If I joined you, I don't think it would be to pretzel."

"That so?" She slowly lowered her legs and then piked, her rounded ass near his groin. Then she spread her legs so they were on either side of his and kicked into a handstand. Damn. She made him stupid-hot like a teenager when she pulled stunts like this. And she knew it. Upside down, she looked at him and smiled. Then she spread her legs into the splits.

A dare.

"You are a wicked tease," he whispered, aching for her. He wanted to pull himself out of his jeans and stroke himself while he watched her, but damn, she had to do this out in the open. He closed his eyes. "But my momma raised me right. Work first. Let's get your booth set up."

And then what? He'd bring her to Grey's? Hang with his dad and a bunch of cowboys—many of them friends—and pretend this thing with Piper was casual like it should be? Or leave her alone? Both options sucked.

"Already set up."

She smirked and drew her legs together and came down out of the handstand with total control. She had defined abs, and the toned muscles on her back were cut enough that they played peekaboo no matter what she was doing when she wore her usual racer back or halter tanks and dresses. Boone would never have guessed what a turn-on cut muscles on a woman would be. Piper's dancer body, honed by years of practice, had morphed him into an anatomy whore.

"What? How? When? Baby you don't need to carry all those things. I said I'd be back. I know I'm late, but…"

She turned toward him with that liquid walk and kissed his mouth into silence.

He kissed her back. He'd already felt hot, ready to crawl out of his skin, but now he caught fire. He cupped the back of her head. Tugged out her elastic. Let her silky, fragrant red-gold hair fall all around him. She kissed like she did everything: full-on, warm, sensual, total focus. She made him feel like a god, like he was her whole world.

"When I ordered the table and chair they were advertised as mobile. That means ready to move."

"I like to help you," he confessed like the biggest whipped-ass boyfriend ever. He closed his eyes, leaned his forehead against hers as if that would somehow hide what he felt and what she did to him.

"I know. But a mountain of a man with his clumsy but cute white dog with a tail that wagged like a flag the entire time and his cuter son set everything up before I could do much more than offer them cookies. Oh, and he had a massive hammer looped into his jeans. Like Thor. I like this town."

"Sounds like Colt Wilder and Parker. And he's very married."

Piper rolled her eyes. "Wasn't looking to jump *him*."

The way she emphasized 'him' shattered the last of his control.

"Let's take this inside." Boone pulled her flush to his body, his hand already at the small of her back reeling her in tightly so she could feel what she did to him—far safer than talking about anything that was rolling around his brain like ball bearings.

"One-track mind, cowboy." She smiled and pressed a kiss to his jaw. "I was thinking it would be fun to walk around the town. I was reading more and wanted to see it. The pictures make it look like a movie set." Piper's voice rang with enthusiasm, and Boone felt his quick burst of desire shrivel.

Damn. He'd promised his dad he'd catch a drink with him and talk about the stock he was bringing. He'd promised Piper he would show her around the town.

"Seriously, Boone. I know you said you'd been here before, but Marietta sounds awesome. Practically perfect. Maybe even the cutest place we've been together." She slid her fingers through his. "There's a dessert company, a coffee shop. Even locally made chocolates at a shop named after the mountain." She swung her slim, bare arm wide to point to Copper Mountain. "And you know how you're always teasing me that you'll buy me one of those snap-button, blinged-out western-style shirts? There's a store called Western Wear. I thought I'd buy one, wear one of your buckles and cheer you on from the stands. In the green and gray boots you bought me to 'match my eyes.'" She air quoted him.

God, she was perfect.

But her timing sucked. No. It was his timing. And he had to wrap his head around this—whatever it was—and let her go. He'd been tired of hookups. Lonely, and aching for something he couldn't define. Seeing Piper gliding on the water had been a lightning strike. Spontaneous.

Instead he'd had to go and ruin it by…by…damn he couldn't even go there, couldn't even think those words. He'd just turned twenty-five. Piper was gorgeous, sweet, smart and fun. A great travel companion. He had to leave it at that.

Stick to his plan.

"Sounds good," he hedged and smoothed his hands through her gorgeous red-gold hair because he couldn't help himself. "But I…" Damn, he couldn't even look her in the eye. "I was going to head over to Grey's. Talk to some folks. There's a special ceremony after the parade tomorrow—a dedication because of the fire last year. They're having a complication with the temporary staging area and wanted some help."

That was true, but he still felt guilty because there was more.

"Boone." She slid her arms up so that her hands were at his nape. She played with his hair, and he couldn't help the sigh of pleasure. His eyes drifted shut. Piper always soothed him—when she wasn't jacking him up. "You are always the first to step in and help people. I love that so much about you."

His eyes snapped open. "It's not that big of a deal."

"It is." Her smile was luminous. "People know they can rely on you, even people who just meet you. You fix things—it's your superpower."

He laughed. He felt pretty superpower-less compared to everyone in his family.

"Pretty sure only you'd say that."

Piper kissed the corner of his mouth, and he chased her lips until she sighed and her body went pliant in his arms.

"So Grey's, huh? The first building in town. A former brothel. Of course." She winked. "I trust that's history. Not present." She eyed him, and he felt caught. It would be natural for him to ask her. He always did. Damn he was being dumb. Dumber than dumb. He could hardly hide who he was, what he was from her all weekend.

"Um…Piper, listen…"

"You don't want me to go with you," she interrupted and pulled away.

He immediately felt the distance. And his hands flexed with the effort to not pull her back into his arms.

"No. I do. It's not that."

"Pretty sure it's that, Boone," she said softly. Her gaze held his and he wished she were pissed at him, yelling.

"Go. Go meet whomever you want to meet, Boone. I'd appreciate a heads-up if it's an old or not so old flame."

He felt like she'd struck him. For a moment his jaw was so tight he couldn't unlock it to speak.

"Where the hell did that come from?"

"You've been acting strange all day. Secretive. Hot and cold."

Damn. If that's what a double college degree and a massage certification did for a person, he was in a whole lotta trouble.

"You think I'd do that?" He felt his eyes go squinty. He rarely got pissed but when he did, his brothers and friends had always backed down. "Raw fury" his brother Rohan had dubbed his reaction. "You think I'd meet a woman behind your back?"

Piper drew in a shaky breath. Squared her shoulders. Met his turbulent glare. One more thing to love about her…no. Not love. Like. Admire. He forced himself to calm down. She was brave. Smart and full of courage.

"It happens, Boone. No I don't think that. But you are a beautiful man inside and out. I know a lot of women notice because you're like a magnet wherever you go."

Just like that his tension eased.

"Baby, men aren't beautiful. And you've caused your fair share of whiplash when we go out and dance, especially when we dance."

Grey's had dancing. He loved to dance, but dancing with Piper was an art form. With her he could dance all night. And then when they'd get home to his small trailer, they'd dance in a different way for hours. Sometimes he felt desperate, like he couldn't get close enough, deep enough inside her.

Suddenly he couldn't remember why he didn't want her to go to Grey's.

"And Grey's has dancing." So now, like a total contrary idiot, he wanted to persuade her? He caught her around her small waist, hand flat on the small of her back, and pulled her deep into him. He did a little two-step and a dip. She moved with him. Her hand stroked through his hair, but he could tell her mind was elsewhere.

"Well see," she said. "Maybe later. I'm going to walk around the town." She pulled away casually. She didn't look at him, and Boone felt like he died a little inside. "I'm going to see if there are any community boards where I can post my business cards so if anyone from town wants a quick massage they can find me and get a discount."

"Java Café," he said without thinking. "And the feed store, Big Z's and the library." He caught her staring. "At a guess," he inserted.

Piper looked suspicious. He had a wild urge to scoop her up and take her into the trailer, blow off his dad and the rodeo committee and just spend the afternoon with Piper because their time was running out.

"Have fun," she said and the distance in her crystal-clear eyes chilled him to his marrow.

"It's just a beer," Boone said. "And a round of pool maybe."

"Boone, I am not your mother."

"Let's go to dinner," he said recklessly. "Meet me at Grey's after you put up some of your cards. Or take a quick look around the town, and I'll help you take your cards around before dinner."

Stupid. Everyone knew him in town. Everyone. Yeah he'd been a youth rodeo champion like a lot of other teens. But his dad had been rodeo-star famous. And his mom had been one of the most celebrated and beautiful and talented rodeo queens in Montana. Rodeo royalty. His entire family was amazing. He was happy for all of them. Thrilled and proud. But he needed to step up.

"We'll see how you feel, Boone. Have fun."

She hopped up the two stairs to the trailer and closed the door. Locked it. Boone stared at the door, knowing this was the first part of goodbye.

Chapter Four

Piper entered the Copper Mountain Chocolate shop, closed her eyes and inhaled deeply. The smell was dark and rich and sweet and seemed to wrap around her somewhere deep inside. When she'd walked into the shop, there'd been three women in copper-colored aprons putting milk and dark chocolate cowboy boots in little bags with bows and larger selections in cute boxes.

Piper realized the conversation had ceased.

Her eyes snapped open. The three women were staring at her, smiling.

"Ooops." Piper laughed. "Busted."

"No, I still do that," the woman with gorgeous red hair that was pinned back from her fine features said. "Every day. It never gets old. You in town for the rodeo?"

Piper nodded, a strange lump in her throat. The women were co-workers and they seemed happy, friends even. What would it be like to have colleagues who were friends? She'd moved too much to ever have that. And when she'd danced professionally for two years, they'd always been competing for roles so you could never really trust anyone.

Like every other business, the window of the chocolate shop was decorated for the rodeo. Probably the women were planning an event after the parade tomorrow. Piper had seen the parade advertised as she walked around the town, pinning up a few of her cards.

She'd been surprised at how agreeable everyone had been. And how they'd been curious about her. She'd even met the owner of the hardware store, Big Z's, Paul Zabrinski, who had cleared out a space for her and had asked her how she liked touring with the rodeo and whether she'd grown up on a ranch. He'd made her feel so welcome with his easy manner and interest when she'd told him of some of the places she'd lived and traveled to both growing up and as a dancer.

"Sounds like a dream," he'd said as Piper had prepared to leave. "But this business keeps me grounded. My family's here. My wife, Bailey, and kids, friends. This is where I belong and how I like it."

Piper was starting to like Marietta too, the little she'd seen. And the chocolates looked and smelled divine.

"Yes, I am," Piper answered the red-haired woman. "I'm a masseuse traveling with the rodeo." It made her sound more professional and less head over heels than if she said she was traveling with her boyfriend. The three faces continued to smile at her. She peered into the display case. "I love the cowboy boot chocolates. Well, I love everything cowboy lately."

"Don't we all. I'm Sage. I used to barrel race. Now I'm a chocolatier and have opened a chocolate shop."

"What's that song called? 'Save A Horse (Ride A Cowboy)'?" Piper said feeling comfortable with the three women—way too comfortable because the minute the words popped out of her mouth she slapped her hand over it. The words sounded so sexual when out in the open like that, and Marietta was a small town. Probably far more conservative than she was accustomed to.

But no worries, the three women laughed.

"Got that right," one of them said.

"We've all got cowboys so we know how it is," Sage said. "Being on tour is a hard life. I prefer having a home and my family and friends around me and now my store. So there is life after the rodeo in case you're wondering."

Piper had wondered. A lot. But it didn't seem fair to hope for Boone to change, to give up his career. He hadn't talked about after—what he wanted, his dreams, his family. She just knew his dad had been a cowboy and that he'd grown up on a Montana ranch. She wished he'd talk more about his family, had even hoped to meet them, but Boone tended to stay in the moment. Besides, maybe his relationship with his father was as fraught as hers.

And Piper hadn't exactly told Boone she wanted to find a place where she belonged. Create her own family and circle of friends. She hadn't wanted to scare him away, but not talking about the future got harder and harder because she couldn't imagine hers without him in it.

Almost blindly she chose chocolates—milk and dark chocolate cowboy boots and salted caramels with lavender just because they sounded so gourmet.

She even bought a hot chocolate because it was "world famous."

She sipped the hot chocolate. It was delicious, but not enough to soothe the ache that had opened inside of her today when Boone had become so distant. She knew what that meant. Time to be on her way. Make her own plans. She had a dream. She couldn't let a cowboy who loved the open road steal it from her.

Piper waved goodbye and pushed her sunglasses on her face, more to hide her stupid tears than to block the afternoon sun, as she stepped out onto the sidewalk. She tucked her chocolates into her leather backpack and scanned Main Street.

It really looked too cute to be believed. Almost like a Hollywood set of an old western town, but updated. She could see the historic courthouse at the end of the street, facing the town, as if protecting it from whatever might come. She wanted to explore. The rodeo-themed window displays looked so sweet. She loved the history that seeped from every building, but being honest with herself, she really wanted to see the town with Boone. She loved hanging out with him—window-shopping, hiking, swimming, eating at a late-night diner. He made everything fun. And even this picturesque town with the friendly people, historic architecture, breath-taking scenery and alluring shops felt flat without him.

But she was likely going to have to get used to being on her own again.

"Who knows," she whispered to herself but in some ways she felt like she was sharing her thoughts with the twin brother who'd died before he'd been born, "maybe this town needs a massage therapist."

She'd seen Grey's Saloon when she'd made her first pass on one side of the street. She'd wanted to turn in, but didn't feel welcome. And she wasn't quite ready to face the end of the road with Boone. The Western Wear store also caught her eye. Boone had often teased her about the western-style snap shirts. It had been a bit of a back and forth flirty game with them because she would steal his shirts and wear them.

Maybe it was time to get one and make some of her own memories. She'd fallen in love with the west—Montana even more than Colorado and Wyoming. When she allowed herself to think about the end of the tour, she fantasized about settling in a small town with friendly people and views that went on forever. Only in her dreams, she wasn't alone.

BOONE WAS RESTLESS, not unusual for him, but normally he contained it better. He wasn't a kid anymore getting sent to the principal because he couldn't keep his ass planted in a small, hard, blue plastic chair. Even playing a couple games of pool and catching up with a few friends and his father and a few ranchers also on the rodeo committee, he couldn't help how his eyes kept straying toward the swinging double doors of the saloon.

Piper should be here. It was nearly happy hour and a young bluegrass band was jamming—taking the piss-poor time slot just to get in some playing time.

Piper would love the music. And she would always dance with him, her supple body close, her mouth curved in a smile just for him.

"Sure you don't want another beer?" his dad asked.

Boone shrugged a no. "Only one a day during a riding weekend," was his standard reply, and usually he stuck to the rule. He'd always felt a bit virtuous that he took good care of himself on the tour until two years ago he'd met world champion American Extreme Bull Rider, Kane Wilder, who'd been buying up a lot of ranch land around Marietta with his three brothers, Colt, Laird and Luke. Kane was going into a joint venture with Boone's dad. Kane didn't eat any sugar, dairy or grains and didn't drink alcohol, not even one beer when he was on tour. Boone wasn't that hard-core but he had made some nutritional changes with Piper's encouragement, and he'd noticed a difference already in his healing time. Fewer aches and less stiffness.

"Heard we got a new saddle bronc competitor joining

the tour this weekend. CJ Cooper," his dad said.

Boone knew his dad well enough to know that there was more, so he waited.

"A cowgirl."

"Seriously?" Boone's face split in a smile. "That's gonna scald some nuts." Boone finished the last dregs of his beer and placed the empty on a ledge. "That's good. Real good for the sport."

"Thought so too. About time."

"Have you seen her ride? Think she can beat Jesse Carmody? He's riding fierce this season."

"That he is. No idea. We'll get our first glimpse of her skills Saturday along with everyone else, but she qualified for her pro-card. Hope she sticks it. Good role model for kids, boys and girls."

Boone nodded, his mind already drifting away from the conversation, but he tried to rally so his dad wouldn't think something was wrong, which it was.

"Jesse will handle it better than some if she tops the leaderboard."

His dad snorted a laugh of agreement. Then he took a long swallow of his beer, clearly weighing his words, and Boone braced himself.

"Season's treatin' you good," his dad commented after a long pause, where Boone tried to keep his eyes on the game and not on the double doors of the entrance.

Not like last year.

That's what Boone heard, but that was on him. His dad didn't make personal digs. He said what he meant to your face. Still the comment made Boone's gaze flick to his father, away from his deep study of the front doors. His dad never talked tour. Boone hadn't figured out if it was because he didn't want to put extra pressure on him, or if he was getting impatient for Boone to call it a day and come back home to work full time on the ranch. Boone loved working the ranch, but it was the Telford Family Ranch, potent with family history and his father's accomplishments.

Because he was Boone Telford, he'd always have a place there. But he hadn't done anything special to earn it. Just been born a Telford.

"'S alright."

His dad laughed. "You know you still got a bed at the house."

"Trailer suits me fine."

He got the look. The 'your mom wants her son home' look.

"Makes more sense for me to be closer," he defended. "Plus you and Mom are involved in a lot of the social events this weekend. And Riley's singing at the grand reopening ceremony. You'll see more of me in town."

"You haven't been back this summer."

His father saw too much, and Boone felt ten again and wished he'd taken his dad up on the beer. But he knew if he kept silent the moment, such as it was, would pass.

"You good?"

Boone watched the pool game and jerked his head 'yes.'

"Hoping you'll stop at the ranch on your way out," his dad finally said into the fraught silence. "Got some equipment that needs your magic touch."

"Of course."

"Wilders have a few things they'd like you to look at on their ranch."

Boone nodded. Anything mechanical he could handle. His life, though? He seemed always poised to fuck it up.

"They've been waiting a while."

Boone switched his gaze to the pool game.

"And I'll need your help with the rodeo sound system, later today or early tomorrow, and part of the stage is giving us fits." His dad didn't change tone, but Boone knew he was confused and disappointed. And fishing for answers.

"Sure." Boone shot his dad a look. "You only claim me for my hands and inability to say no."

If his dad replied, he didn't hear it because right then Piper flowed through the double doors. They immediately locked eyes, and it was just like the first time. Every time he saw her it was like the first time—that sense of falling, of breathlessness, and of a recognition that went soul-deep even as it made no sense.

"'Scuze me. Going to ask a girl to dance." Boone pulled away from his wall slouch, handed his pool cue to a cowboy who'd been watching and walked toward Piper with purpose.

Damn. She'd bought a western shirt. A green and tan and pink plaid one, and she was wearing the jeans he'd bought her in Missoula with the bling on the back pockets that accented the sweet curve of her butt that always drove him to distraction. The room and the band and his father and friends all faded way.

Was Piper wearing a bra or a tank under the shirt? She had the neck open almost to her cleavage. What the hell was she trying to do, kill him? He was so intent on watching her watch him that he didn't notice Dean Maynard, two longnecks dangling from his fingers, reach her first.

He couldn't hear what Dean said, but he'd seen him in action way too many times. And Maynard had been on the tour long enough to know, absolutely know that Piper was his.

"Back off," he said rudely, cutting in to put his body between Dean and Piper.

"Soft and pretty boys aren't my type, Telford," Dean sneered. "So get the fuck out of my face. If you're gonna let your girl walk into a bar alone lookin' like that, you're gonna get some competition, and I know you aren't always on top of your game to stick the ride."

Boone felt the adrenaline, already surging, slam through him like a tsunami.

"Boone." Piper was now between him and Dean, her arms looped around his neck and her body pressed to his. "Let's dance."

He was shaking with the unspent adrenaline. Maynard's lip curled, mocking him. Daring him. Hell, yeah, Dean wanted him to throw the first punch. That could get him cut from the tour faster than low scores. Dean was used to being on top, and this year he was falling in the rankings, fast. And drinking heavily.

"Telford, she's got you tied down faster than any calf you ever roped."

"Ignore him," Piper said, pulling him further into the bar toward the band and away from the entrance. She stroked the back of his neck with her fingers. Boone breathed away the need for action and leaned down and pressed his forehead to hers. Piper always centered him.

"I think you're going to have to add caveman to your résumé," Piper said lightly.

"Starting to feel like I might." He spun her in fairly tight circles despite the fact that they were the only ones dancing. His hand skimmed along her waist and rested on her hip. He wanted to touch the bling on her butt, but he knew his dad and men who'd known him his entire life were watching and wouldn't let that action go unremarked.

"You bought a western shirt," he said.

"You like?"

"Pretty crazy about it with you in it. You wearing a bra?"

She smiled mysteriously. "You'll have to find out, cowboy."

His hand smoothed down her back, and he sucked in a

breath. "Pretty sure you're going to kill me before the short round on Sunday."

"You're tough."

"What took you so long? I've been waiting."

"You've been playing pool." Her eyes, always so mystical to him with the way they changed from green to gray and back again depending on her mood and the light, seemed to laugh at him. "Boys and their sticks."

"I can show you mine if you want," he whispered in her ear. Naughty, wanting to make her laugh. Instead she bit her plump lower lip that had starred in so many fantasies these past months and looked up at him. Uncertain.

He felt something strange wash over him. Icy cold and in a wave that felt like it could toss him off-balance. It was almost like the time his little sister Riley had fallen off her horse when it had spooked. Instead of running off, it had danced, agitated next to her, and he'd hurtled the arena fence, feeling like he couldn't move fast enough.

"Piper?"

She didn't answer, but she nestled closer, her cheek against his sternum, over his heart.

She was close. Way too close. No way would his dad not notice—and wonder. She had her thumbs hooked in his back pockets, her body glued to his, moving with him. And it felt damn perfect. And Boone didn't have the heart or the balls to peel her off him.

He avoided looking at his dad, as he guided Piper around

the small dance floor in a slow two-step only with no turns or promenade. The song was a dreamy ballad, and it ended way too soon.

"You have fun in town?" he asked over the last chord as it faded into silence.

"I walked along a part of the Main Street, and it's really called that. Main Street. It's like a movie set. So cute. Everyone is so friendly. I put up cards at Big Z's and the feed store and Western Wear and the coffee shop like you suggested. I also bought you some chocolate cowboy boots for later if we work up an appetite."

"Lots of ways to do that on and off the dance floor."

She playfully deepened her hip swing against his. Laughed when she felt his instant response.

"You found Sage's did you?" He tried to keep his mind G rated.

"How'd you know her name?"

"You read to me all about the town, the history, the parade, the picnic, the steak dinner."

"Don't forget the pancake breakfast."

"Never miss it."

Lightning really needed to strike him down.

The band broke into an upbeat version of Chris Stapleton's "Parachute" and Boone lead Piper around the floor fast with a lot of flair and finesse not often seen outside the competitions. He felt his mood improving. He'd always loved to dance and the fact that Piper had been a dancer before she'd studied massage meant that she matched his energy and loved it as much as he did.

He loved how her slim, supple body felt moving with his. She made him feel strong and certain of who he was and his place in the world. But then reality continued to crash back through the chute, and he was left feeling like he needed to be more…more something.

After their third song, he was aware that the pool game had finished. His dad and another local rancher and stock contractor, Luke Wilder, sauntered back to the bar, deep in conversation with Luke's wife, Tanner. She grinned, pulled off her hat with a dramatic sweeping motion, her bright red ponytail spilled over one slim shoulder. "Hey, Boone," she called out. "Enjoy your dance because I expect one of my beautiful bulls to toss your ass off Saturday so you'll be too sore to show off your dancing skills at the steak dinner and dance."

Luke jerked a nod in his direction, failing to hide his smile.

"You'll be disappointed." Boone couldn't let that slide, but this was all going to go badly soon. He needed to explain to Piper and not make a big deal about it. She'd understand. And it wasn't like he had to make some huge ultimatum this weekend. Rodeo weekends were the worst time to make any life changes. Distractions led to serious injuries. Even death. He needed to do his job—win or place high in his events, earn some money and help his father ensure that the opening went well tomorrow.

Time for decisions Sunday when he headed home.

He just wanted more time with Piper.

"You're thinking enough for an entire school," Piper said, looking into his eyes.

"I'm thinking maybe we should get out of here," he said ruefully because that part was at least true. If he continued to dance with Piper, his dad would definitely know it was far more than casual. He was practically flashing a neon sign as it was.

"All you need to do is ask."

"Let's go." He spun her toward the door, slipped an arm around her waist and then walked out fast. He raised his hand in the air in a general 'see y'all later.'

His dad would probably be shocked at his abrupt departure with a girl, but hell, he was twenty-five. Cowboys on the tour hooked up all the time for the weekend. Or the night. Or an afternoon. But Piper was not a hookup, and it burned a little that his dad might think she was.

THE MINUTE THE late-afternoon sun slanted across them when the swinging doors of Grey's Saloon swung shut behind them, Boone pulled Piper into a tight hug. He hadn't meant to. Total reflex. Piper sighed and looped her arms around his neck, her fingers already playing in his hair, which sent shivers down his spine. He didn't think it was possible but he hardened even more.

"Sometimes I wish I could just hold you without that part of me interrupting," he confessed.

Piper stood on her tiptoes. Her soft laughter teased his neck as she nuzzled him and then pressed soft kisses against his jaw.

"I'm addicted to your interruptions. Trailer?" she questioned.

Hell, he wasn't even sure he could make it there. She was moving against him subtly as she kissed him, and then her teeth caught his lower lip. Boone groaned low in his throat. He sounded like an animal. He felt like one, but they were on Main Street Marietta and it was still daylight. Then she stood on her tiptoes, angling her body so that his erection pressed against her taut abdomen.

"Baby, you are not making this easy," he hissed even as he kissed her back, feeling his hunger grow. He wanted to let it slip its leash.

"Wasn't trying to."

"Let's get you fed," he said trying to think of something practical, mundane, not Piper naked spread across his navy and taupe comforter.

She slipped her hands down his pockets and grabbed his ass.

"Sounds like a plan. I love what's on the menu."

He marshaled discipline he didn't know he had—maybe helped by the fear that his dad could walk out any minute with a handful of the rodeo committee members—men he'd known all his life—and he didn't want to be groping Piper in the doorway.

"Guacamole," he said a little desperately, his brain barely engaged, and why he'd jumped on that, he had no idea. Boone didn't eat a lot of green things, and when he did, it was because he was trying to please Piper, and this year he'd been more focused on his health for the long haul. "Mexican. There's a new Mexican restaurant in town." Hell if he could remember the name right now.

"Rosita's," Piper said, pulling away from him. "I saw it during my walk."

Boone gulped in some air, wishing it were arctic so he could cool down and drag his mind out of the bedroom.

"But I wanted to walk around town with you," she said softly, scuffing the toe of her green boot along the sidewalk. "But since you've competed here, you've probably already explored everything."

The sweet innocence of her comment ripped through him and lodged hot and malevolent like a bullet in his gut.

"Piper," he whispered. He had to tell her. He needed to tell her.

But then what?

He'd hurt her.

And he'd have to explain something he didn't really understand. This need that burned.

Or they'd fight. She'd leave.

Damn, he was not ready for that. He felt a million miles from ready. And this was his hometown. He had to keep his focus on his events. Making up for last year. Not get sucked up in a drama of his own making.

"Maybe after dinner we can walk down Main Street in the dark with the stars out and the courthouse lit up. I bet it will be magical."

He just stared down at her—her upturned face so loving and accepting. The smallest moments made her happy. He was the most undeserving idiot in Montana. Hell, the whole US.

He had to clear his throat to speak around the lump there. Still he was hoarse. "You're the magic one, Piper."

She slipped her hand in his and they started to walk down Main Street toward Rosita's. Boone hadn't been in before. His oldest brother Witt had told him about it. He and his wife, Miranda, met there often for dinner after work with their adopted daughter.

He hoped tonight wasn't one of those nights.

"Let's order takeout," he suggested.

Piper's eyes darkened with desire, and he felt an answering throb thump through him. "With extra guacamole."

"Since making guac is practically a religion for you, and you eat it with baked kale, I doubt this is going to pass muster," he teased.

"You never know. These small family-run restaurants are the backbone of America. I saw a diner in town. Main Street

Diner. On Main Street. I love the lack of pretension. This is America. Something I feel like I've been looking for all my life."

Boone didn't quite know what to make of that.

"My dad, the colonel. He served America—the people of America, but we were rarely in America. The Americans I met were Army or contractors and their families. I always wondered what small-town America was like. What my dad was fighting for."

Boone nodded, thinking of his brother, Rohan, and his service, the places he'd been, and the places Piper had lived. He probably couldn't find all of them on a map.

They ordered takeout and waited at the bar, holding hands, Piper sipped a margarita and shared it with him while they waited.

Boone paid, frowning when Piper pulled out her wallet. She really should know better than that by now. He wanted to take care of Piper.

She was his. He remembered the wave of possession that had rolled over him on the dance floor at Grey's. He had to stop thinking that way.

"You ordered a lot of guac," the server said with a bright smile as she handed over the bagged-up food. "Want me to slip in an extra order of chips?"

Boone took the bag, opening his mouth to say that more chips would be great, but Piper beat him to it.

"No thank you," Piper said cheerfully already turning to

walk out.

"Why not extra chips?" Boone asked following her. Piper worshipped green food. Chips and salsa was Boone's take me to church moment. And he would happily munch on them every day. Tomatoes were a vegetable. Or were they a fruit? Piper would know.

"Don't need them," Piper said.

"I do."

Piper turned around, her walk a little saucy, and Boone found his eyes riveted on the sway of her hips in the blinged-out jeans—jeans that had caused her to look at him so doubtfully when he'd bought them.

She turned around and blew him a kiss. "The guac is not for the chips."

"Come again?" Boone stopped on the sidewalk.

Piper's eyes sparkled with mischief. She reached into one of the bags and pulled out a container of guac. She popped the lid.

"I've been thinking," she said playfully.

"Always dangerous," Boone shot back.

"I think I've come up with a way to get you to eat more guac," she said, dipping her finger in and smearing a little on her upper lip. Her tongue poked and languidly scooped up the guac. "Mmmmmmmm," she hummed and let her eyes drift shut. She looked like she did before she orgasmed, and Boone could barely walk. Again.

"Let's go." Boone seized her arm and speed-walked down

Main Street, Piper keeping pace, laughing at him.

"Hungry?" she asked.

"Starved."

Chapter Five

BOONE FELT NEARLY desperate by the time they reached the trailer. His hands shook and he fumbled the keys.

"Let me help you." Piper slid around him onto the step.

Some help. On the second step of the trailer her rounded ass brushed against his groin. And she did it on purpose. Her eyes gleamed green as she looked at him over her shoulder.

"Hurry," he hissed.

"Such a rush."

Piper slid the key into the lock.

"I can take all night if you want," Boone promised.

After he made Piper scream. Then took his edge off. Then took care of Sundance for the night.

Piper unlocked the door, but before she could step inside the trailer, he wrapped his arm around her waist and picked her partially up and boosted her into the trailer. And then he slammed the door behind him. Like a savage. Like someone he didn't recognize. And didn't care. He tossed the takeout bag on the table.

"Boone." Piper was already in his arms, and his shirt was

unsnapped and on the floor. "You should eat first. Keep up your stamina."

"Stamina's fine," he said pulling off his T-shirt with his right hand, and tossing it behind him.

"I'll feed you," she whispered, her lips against his chest, the tip of her tongue already working its magic.

"Intend to eat," he said as she grabbed hold of the belt buckle he'd won for steer wrestling at the Wild Horse Stampede in June and walked backward toward the back of the trailer. She shed one boot and then the other without stumbling.

"Pretty fancy move," he said, thinking he was way behind since she was fully clothed and he'd tossed his hat and shirt and Piper's dexterous fingers had already opened his belt buckle as he walked her back. Or was she pulling him? He loved how she was so into his body. So into him.

"You like that move?" Her voice had gone totally husky now, and her eyes that had stayed riveted south of his buckle flicked up to his face. "How 'bout this one?"

One leg slid between his, and crooked around his knee. Holding his shoulders, she twisted him around and the pressure on the back of his knee took him down on the bed.

"Not going to object," he said pulling on her thick ponytail enough so that he could tug off the elastic. Her hair fell around him and he briefly closed his eyes savoring all that silk and her lemon and honeysuckle scent. Who would have guessed he'd be such a scent slut? "Although that slick move has me thinking."

"About?" Her voice edged with excitement as she straddled him, her knees wide and her hands splayed along his hips.

"Ropes," he said.

He'd shocked her. Piper's pupils flared and her breath caught.

"I used to be part of a team," he said. "Top five most rodeos. Still pretty good roping calves."

"So now I'm a calf?" She nipped his pec hard enough to make him wince. "Does that line go over well with the bunnies? Get you a line outside your trailer?"

"Been known to make a few hearts flutter," he admitted. "But I'm not interested in a line, Piper."

She slid her body down his, her eyes slumberous and dark with desire.

Damn, she made him crazy. He'd never even thought of roping a woman before, but with Piper, she made him feel like anything was possible. Every day was an adventure.

And that was the end of his thought as she leaned over him and with her teeth caught the edge of his 501s and tugged. One button. Then another. And another.

"You remembered," she said softly and kissed her way down the narrow blond arrow of hair below his navel. His erection unencumbered by Jockeys, sprang free.

"Still think commando makes me a perve."

He was already leaking and at full attention when Piper

released the last button of his jeans.

"No, it makes me so hot for you." She did a slow swipe with her tongue around his sensitive tip. "Especially when I see you talking to other people, knowing you're mine and always ready for me."

He groaned and swore as she engulfed him with her hot, sweet mouth. The things she did with her tongue were X-rated, and Boone fought the urge to thrust into her moist heat. Piper was strong, but so delicately made. He was always afraid he'd hurt her.

"And when you're working with Sundance or fixing something with the truck or trailer or helping another cowboy, I love to think about standing behind you and unbuttoning your jeans, just a few buttons to release you and then I'd stroke you until you're hard."

That would take about half a second. Boone gripped the comforter and bit back a moan.

"My hand would be soft, but the denim rough against your swollen cock."

The visuals she created drove him insane.

Sometimes she'd talk dirty to him when they'd be on the highway, and he'd have to find a place to pull over.

"And then when you're working on Sundance's tack or even better your ropes, and I think about you being commando, it makes me want to kneel in front of you while you are working the rosin into your ropes, getting it all warm and sticky. And your leather glove is cupping my breasts, pinching my nipples."

"Jesus, Piper."

He was going to come and they'd barely started.

"And I fantasize about licking you when you are strapping on your chaps getting ready to compete. Tasting you right there when your name is called that you're up next."

Holy fuck.

He wasn't going to survive.

But if she could actually do that, he'd die happy. And likely be arrested and put in jail.

"Not realistic," he gritted trying to hold on to his sanity.

He'd seen more than one cowboy caught up in their hold rope and dragged half around the arena, jeans torn off, nothing but chaps and their Fruit of the Looms hiding their rod, reel and ass from Internet sensation. He wasn't going to go bare-assed in front of a grandstand full of fans.

"This is my fantasy you're starring in." Piper leaned away from him, and he caught her hair.

She smiled. His heart stuttered in his chest.

"I'm coming back," she promised. "Just another idea. Just for you. Only for you, Boone."

He let her go while an idea of his own, rolling Piper beneath him and taking her hard and fast until she screamed, burned his brain. Then he'd go slow. Take her all night.

Then Piper was back. Her small weight nestled between his thighs.

"Mmmmmm," she hummed along his cock, her breath

warm, and he felt the vibration to his toes. "I love the way you taste," she whispered. "And I'm so hungry." She took another swipe. "Are you hungry, Boone?"

"Killing me, Piper." He wrapped his arm under hers and pulled her up on top of his body.

"Why the fuck are you still wearing clothes?"

"This is my time to play." She wiggled away from him so her lush mouth was poised above his straining cock.

"You didn't answer my question," she breathed against his length. Then she sucked one of his tight balls into the heat of her mouth and rolled it around, and he squeezed his eyes shut against the white light of bliss that seemed to sear his retinas.

Like he could remember anything when Piper got him so jacked up. Had she asked him anything?

"Are you hungry?"

"I want to be inside you," he growled, at the end of his rope. "Fucking now."

"So savage. Impatient." She drew out each syllable, and Boone briefly thought if she had any idea what he really wanted to do to her, savage would be an understatement.

"Let me see if you are ready, mmmmmmm." Piper mused, her lips a warm murmur.

Boone was beyond ready. Every nerve in his body shouted, desperate for her next move, but it was killing him, *killing him* to give up so much control.

Piper never did what he expected. He nearly came off the

bed when something cold touched his dick.

"You didn't dare." He sat up, completely shocked, but also, more than a little turned on.

She lay between his legs. And before he fully registered that she'd dabbed guacamole on him, Piper's hot mouth engulfed him. The moist heat of her mouth and the stroking of her tongue through the suction, and the combination of hot and cold nearly blew off the top of his head.

There had never been anyone like Piper in his life.

He wanted to touch her so badly. It was a fever, the longing to feel the play of her muscles under his palms and fingers. Her back fascinated him. So narrow, but defined. Straight. Graceful. Like an anatomy text from high school.

Sometimes he'd pull back the covers when she slept just to watch her breathe.

Now he watched her take him into her mouth, her focus absolute, and he felt like he was on a precipice. Jump with Piper. Or stand there numb, forever on the edge alone. Lost.

"Piper." He sighed her name to anchor himself.

Her tongue twizzled around his aching shaft while her mouth worked him in and out and it was only a few minutes before he knew he wouldn't be able to last.

He caught her body and lifted her. Her face was stamped with passion and he felt like his heart just seized. "You crank me up so fast." He kissed her hard. His tongue traced the seam of her lips and she let him in instantly. "I want to make it good for you too, baby."

"You always do," she said.

"Damn, you going for some perfect award?"

He'd been joking, his palms already on her hips, his fingers easing down the denim. An expression skittered across her face that he didn't quite understand, but his attention was immediately riveted by the pale pink stretchy lace thong panties she wore.

"Yup, perfect," he breathed, wondering how he'd find the control to take them off without ripping them. He'd ripped her clothes in the past. Too eager. Too crazy for her. Piper deserved more care. Slower. More foreplay.

"You always wanted me to wear one of these snaps shirts," she prompted when he continued to stare at her like he was viewing a holy relic.

Boone swallowed hard. He'd always imagined popping the snaps. Flinging off the shirt who knows where, but instead he smoothed his thumb across her bottom lip.

"You're beautiful, Piper. Inside and out."

He carefully unsnapped one button. Pressed a chaste kiss on the pale flesh he exposed, and then another snap, another kiss until the shirt gaped open.

Piper's breathing was as ragged as his own, but he forced himself to go slow. Savor.

Like it was the last time.

He stared into her face, stricken by the thought.

But it had to be, right? If not tonight, then tomorrow?

"Boone." She cupped his jaw in her palm. "What is it?"

Her beautiful eyes searched his, and he felt like he could stay like this forever. If he could stop the world. Shut up the voice in his head demanding he achieve something. Do more.

Her thumb stroked along his cheekbone even as her fingers feathered along his jaw.

"You have such beautiful bone structure," she sighed.

"You have beautiful everything."

Piper smiled and rolled her shoulders and the fabric of her shirt slipped down to the bed revealing her small, bare breasts, nipples a dusky pink.

"Beautiful and definitely perfect," he breathed. And he was so very flawed.

He palmed her breasts. Reverent. Tentative like the first time.

Then, like always, he lost himself in the feel and scent and heady responses of Piper's whispered encouragements. She was so sensitive and responsive to his touch that she made him feel like a god.

He kissed his way down her body and ran his finger suggestively along the waistband of her panties.

"I thought this was an equal relationship," he teased. "Why in the hell are you wearing panties?"

"They're pretty. I thought you liked lace and a challenge."

"I like lace on the floor. And any more challenge from you, and I'll have a heart attack."

He nipped her hip. She yipped, and he smiled as he traced the panty line low across her abdomen and around her hips, his tongue playing as she shivered and begged and started to thrash under him.

His fingers skimmed the small flesh-toned patch low on her back just below her panty line. It still humbled him that she had gone to a clinic to get birth control to be with him. He'd been in awe and had gotten an exam himself to prove he was clean, to protect her. He'd always worn condoms. Had never had a relationship long enough to think about not wearing them.

He'd still used condoms with Piper, which she'd questioned, but he'd shrugged it off, still wanting to protect her—double protect her.

"Action, cowboy." She angled herself under his body so that he was lodged at her entrance.

"What is this?" He kissed his way back up her body, hanging on to his control by one fingernail. "A race?"

He supported himself above her using his toes and elbows. His hands speared through her hair and cupped her head. He kissed her, over and over, reverent kisses, growing in passion until he felt drugged.

"Boone, hurry," Piper moaned.

She reached up to grab a condom from the box he kept tucked in the side of the bed. He hesitated.

"It's okay," she said. "I've been using the patch."

He smiled. Kissed her, torn. He'd never been bare with a

woman before. He wanted his first time to be with Piper. But in the end, he quickly rolled on the condom and entered her slowly, wanting to feel everything and see her expression. Piper's eyes and expressive face hid little from him.

He went slow and deep.

"You good, Piper?"

She leaned up and kissed his left pec. "Better than."

She clenched her inner muscles around him rhythmically and a groan ripped out of him. He felt like his eyes rolled to the back of his head.

"You like that?"

"Love it a fuck a lot."

"I love how you feel inside me, Boone."

He held her gaze and let her do the slow and deep rhythmic clench that made him feel like his head was going to explode off his spine.

He breathed her name. "Feels like heaven, Piper. Better than, but I gotta move."

She smiled at him so sweetly his heart broke a little, and her hands smoothed over his shoulders and stroked him like he was precious.

He grabbed her ass and tilted her so that he could slide deeply inside of her over and over again. He tried to keep control. Pull almost all the way out before plunging back in, and was rewarded by Piper's throaty cry. He could feel the build, the fire raging in his balls burning every nerve in his body.

"Boone." Her voice broke. He let her go so that he could slip his hand between their bodies and circle her clit with his thumb. It was like touching a live wire. Her climax exploded with no warning and dragged him with her. Dammit. He didn't want to stop. He never wanted to stop. He pumped into her again and again until he collapsed over her.

She held him close, sweaty and panting. "Every time is the best time," she whispered.

Boone felt his heart slam against hers. Fear and self-loathing clenched his gut. Every time got better, but he told himself he had to make it the last time. He had to let Piper go. He didn't deserve her, not now anyway. What did he have to offer her now except the ranch his parents had established for him before he'd been born? He had no big accomplishments of his own, and Piper had so many.

Before he'd been determined to not disappoint himself. Now the idea of disappointing Piper made him queasy.

He kissed her. "Shower first or eat?"

"Just stay like this a moment." She held him.

"I'm pancaking you," he objected.

"I like all your weight on me. I feel grounded."

"I'm supposed to make you feel like you can fly," he disagreed. "And we're just taking a breather so you should eat while you have a chance."

"In that case let's eat first. I have more plans for that guacamole."

Chapter Six

BOONE AND PIPER stood toward the end of Main Street and watched the parade in full swing Friday midmorning. "I have to go." Boone quickly kissed the top of Piper's head. "I promised I'd help out with a few loose ends for the reopening ceremony of the grandstands. The committee asked me yesterday."

"Oh." Piper turned away from the parade of children carrying colorful signs and pictures proudly proclaiming their 4-H club. "I'll head back with you."

"No need. You don't have any appointments until later this afternoon," Boone said. "Enjoy the parade. Looks like there are a lot of sales at the stores. Have a good time." Boone hesitated a moment. "You could treat yourself—get one of those nail things women like."

Piper stared at him. She hadn't had a mani-pedi in her life and now Boone was sending her off like a kid going to a birthday party? He even pulled out his wallet like he was going to pay.

"I'm not your responsibility, Boone," Piper said. She

wanted them to be equals. Partners. Boone already treated her too often. He liked to buy the groceries, but he did let her do most of the cooking although he always jumped in to help clean up the trailer with her.

"You deserve the best, Piper," Boone said, his expression so earnest, she softened.

"So do you." She smoothed her fingers through his hair. "When do you want to catch up again?" She kept her voice light. He had the right to do what he wanted to do without her playing the role of a clingy girlfriend. "Tonight?"

"I'll find you," Boone said easily, scanning the crowd. Then he turned back toward her. "There's a picnic tonight in the park—local groups barbequing hamburgers and hotdogs and lots of sides."

"Sounds good."

"I'll swing by your tent to see how it's going this afternoon," Boone said. "I've got to get my equipment ready for tomorrow."

Usually Piper helped him with that or sat with him and chatted while he worked, so she pressed her lips together to keep from offering.

"See you then." She smiled and stood on her tiptoes, to kiss his jaw.

He surprised her by holding her tightly.

"Boone?" she asked when the moment stretched out.

"Later." He tipped his hat to her and disappeared into the crowd.

Piper stared after him not sure what to think. He had such a beautiful, rolling gait as he moved through the crowd. She sighed and turned back to the parade. She loved the children and the high school band, and the children's clubs, but the shine seemed to be off the parade now that Boone was gone.

He was shutting her out at the same time he was pulling her close.

Piper had felt shut out her entire life—no close relationship with her father, few close friends because she'd been constantly uprooted. She'd made a promise to herself that she would build a life where she felt she had a purpose and a place and a supportive group of friends and, most important, a family of her own.

Strong intentions, she told herself. But she had to follow through. Not get sucked in by Boone's gorgeous blue eyes, dimpled smile and... She sighed—basically she was sucked in by Boone's everything.

And that had to stop.

She stood, racked with indecision as the parade began to wind down. She knew she had to think of her next move. She wasn't ready to give up hope, but she had to get Boone to open up and tell her what was bothering him, and also what he thought about their future—a future neither of them had planned on.

It had been so crazy impulsive to accept his invitation to travel on the rodeo circuit for the summer. But for Piper, it had been a no-brainer opportunity. She was young. No concrete plans. No place to be. No one expecting her. Boone had been handsome and friendly and sexy, and the way he'd looked at her—like she held the sun and moon and had scattered the stars, had lured Piper like nothing else.

She hadn't had a lot of admiration in her life.

And she'd wanted to be one of those young, independent women who could have a hot and exciting fling for a few weeks or a month or two and then walk away with a smile and a lot of pleasant and sexy memories.

Only it had been clear to her, for a while, that she was not going to walk away heart whole or with a fond farewell smile.

"Chocolate," she said to herself. That would nudge her endorphins to the rescue.

And then she could… Piper gnawed on her lower lip in indecision. Maybe she'd get a blowout for her hair so she'd look her best for the picnic tonight. She'd seen an adorable bright pink house on Church Avenue with a sign announcing The Wright Salon. Anything that pink had to be fun. And cheerful. And if this was the end of her and Boone, at least she'd look good in his rearview mirror.

"Pull it together," she ordered. It was unlike her to be so gloomy, and she was pretty certain tears wouldn't cause a cowboy to stay.

It didn't take Boone much time to fix the sound system. He had extra wires in his tool case, cleaned off some corrosion, fixed a few loose connections and then jury-rigged a couple of different speakers with his laptop. He also made a list and priced out the repairs the rodeo committee needed to make and compared it to a new PA system.

"We sure do miss you, son," Travis McMahon, one of rodeo committee members instrumental in spearheading the fundraising for the repairs, sighed. "I know your dad keeps hoping each year is your last on the tour, but your stats are the best they've ever been. Hard to give up the glory."

"Not so sure about the glory, Mr. McMahon," Boone said testing the system one last time, and then he climbed out of the sound booth. "But I sure do love pitting my wits and strength against the broncs and bulls, and I love competing against the other cowboys." He especially loved competing against Cody Starr on the bulls. He was catching up to him in the stats this season.

"I know you young fellas. Adrenaline junkies and think you're immortal. Well, you're not." He held on to Boone's shoulder. "And I know you got a lot of pretty gals after you, but don't leave it too long, son. You want to be able to walk away while you still can—while you got something to walk toward. Your dad needs you home, son. You've got a legacy to build on to."

"Yes, sir," Boone said automatically.

It was his father's legacy. Not his.

"Now you said something about the stage wasn't sitting right?"

And as a distraction, that worked better than most.

An hour later, Boone was standing at the front of a crowd clapping madly as his sister took the small stage in front of the rodeo grounds. She sang an a cappella version of "America the Beautiful" that was so moving. Boone couldn't believe that was his little sis.

Travis McMahon spoke briefly, and then his dad took the stage and didn't look at the notes he'd made for his speech. He seemed completely natural and in his element. He praised how the town had come together to rebuild the grandstand, and repair and improve the fairground's outbuildings so that the rodeo facilities were better than ever.

Boone was proud of his dad. He whistled through his teeth when his dad was done and hugged his mom when she and Riley sidled up next to him.

"Hey, stranger." Riley hit his arm. "Heard you were dancing with a beautiful girl at Grey's yesterday and then ran off with her over your shoulder."

"Actually it was two women," Boone deadpanned.

"And that you kissed her."

"Keep going only keep it G for Mom."

"As if." Riley laughed. "You haven't had a G rating since puberty. Girls have been chasing you since you were ten. I was just relieved that for once you were doing the chasing."

"Stop fishing." Boone didn't look at his sister, but she

was shifting her weight up and down to the balls of her feet like she did when she was excited, and her deep blue eyes shone.

He could feel his mom looking at him. "Your father said you looked quite taken with her. What's her name?"

Boone opened his mouth to make an off-hand remark. But nothing came out. He didn't want to dismiss Piper like she was nothing to him. And he'd never lied to his mom about anything as far as he could remember. But just the way she was leaning in intently and Riley was clearly eager for more information reinforced why he'd kept Piper to himself.

"Heard she was a redhead."

"Strawberry blonde," his mom corrected.

"You two sound like middle school girls," Boone said, putting the kibosh on their teasing. "I need to work on my flank straps."

"Is that what you're calling a date now? Coward," Riley called after him. "At least send me the wedding invitation. I'll sing."

Boone raised his hand high, threatening to flip his sister and her curiosity off.

"Boone Huntingdon Telford don't you dare," his mother called out behind him, and he heard her and his sister laugh.

He couldn't help but laugh himself. He'd missed his family. He'd never been away from them so long, and now that he was back home, he was anxious to get out to the ranch and dig into his chores.

But that was more time away from Piper.

Idiot.

Damn. His head felt screwed on backward and his insides turned out. He just needed to get out of his head. Get on the back of a bronc so he could focus on what was important. Survival. Not to keep thinking about tomorrow or the day after.

He'd never planned for the future. Why should he? This feeling slushing inside him, this worry, this doubt sucked.

He made it to the stock building and immediately felt his cares fall away as he brushed Sundance and used a pick on his hooves. Taking care of Sundance was soothing, but he was used to doing so much more—working daily with cattle and horses, and now his mom had a small herd of alpacas that she was using for their wool—Serena Zabrinski had gotten her started and his dad would often end phone calls with the name of the latest alpaca herd member.

They were stinkin' cute with their googly eyes and goofy grins, but cowboys did not herd alpacas. And with alpacas, you needed llamas, and his dad had funny stories about them as well.

Taryn Telford was enjoying his ranch—living the life he wanted with his wife. He didn't technically need Boone home. His dad had ranch hands. It was not as if Boone were leaving him overworked. Plus, his dad was in the prime of health since he'd healed from his injury from a bull this past winter.

Boone headed back out to the lot set up for the competitors to stay during the rodeo. It was getting crowded, and Boone felt the anticipation building.

"Boone." He hadn't been paying attention, but a large hand was thrust into his and pumped. "Kane Wilder. Been partnering up some with your dad. We met at the rodeo two years ago."

Boone looked into familiar pale blue, almost silver eyes and nearly laughed. Like Kane Wilder had to introduce himself to anyone in Montana or to anyone on the rodeo circuit anywhere in the world. Kane was a world champion bull rider on the American Extreme Bull Riding Tour. His skills were as famous as his face and his smile. He'd had another killer year and word was he was sinking most of his prize money and endorsement money into buying up land and stock and bringing the new Wilder Dreams ranch up to top standards.

"Good to see you, again. Thanks for all the efforts you've given to rebuild the grandstand and the rodeo grounds and outbuildings," Boone said sincerely. His father had been so impressed by Kane. They were practically best buddies now that they were working together on breeding bulls. Kane was still very active on the tour so Boone's dad was doing most of the work, but Kane's two sisters-in-law and brother Luke were working with Boone's dad.

Kane waved his hand dismissively. "It was a group effort. My part was small. You going on any of the stock-buying trips with your dad and Tanner?" he asked, naming his sister-in-law who had already started making a name for her bulls before she lost her ranch and most of her stock due to her father's illness, addiction and gambling debts.

"This winter yes," Boone said. "But I'll be heading out again spring and summer for the rodeo."

Kane nodded. "Your dad values your opinion. Hoping you'll be on board full time next year."

Everybody did. But him.

"You'll be back in the AEBR Tour, right?" Boone deflected and ignored Kane's searching gaze. "You're still on top."

Kane shrugged fluidly. "That's the trick isn't it? To quit when you're ahead. I heard there was a masseuse with the Montana tour this summer. Usually Sky helps me to stretch out each morning, but this is her big weekend with her statue dedication and the press and her agent and manager Jonas are out for the dedication, so I'm trying to keep out of her way."

Boone respected Kane for that.

"Yeah, there is a masseuse. She's damn good. Piper," he said. "Piper Wiley. Her tent is the blue one right over there." Boone started toward Piper's tent that was set up near the entrance of the changing area a short ways away. "If the door is tied back she's open. I'm not sure if she's working now, but she has an appointment book. I'll…"

Boone didn't finish his sentence. Piper was there at the

mouth of her tent waiting, stylish and sexy in skinny jeans and an off-the-shoulder floral blouse that skimmed her slim curves. She smiled at seeing him, but immediately her warm gaze moved to Kane, and her smile was more professional.

Piper ducked back in the tent and came out wearing the soft white wrap jacket she wore when she was working.

She should have looked plain, but no, Piper rocked that look too.

She approached them, smiling professionally again, and held out her hand to Kane. Boone felt like a stranger and that chilled him to the bone.

Kane introduced himself, and asked about availability of a massage.

"Now's good." Piper untied the side of her tent that kept a flap open as a door.

"See you later, Boone." The fabric swished shut behind her.

"SHIRT ON OR shirt off?" Kane asked.

"Your choice," Piper said. "Normally massage works better if I don't have fabric in the way, but a lot of you cowboys are tough. It took me two months to get any of them to lie on the table. It was only the chair." Piper found herself smiling even though her heart hadn't quite settled down from seeing Boone. It was ridiculous to be nervous. But it was even dumber to not talk things out with him. She should trust him enough to ask what was bothering him. Or to tell him her feelings. If he ran, well, at least she would know her feelings weren't returned.

"Shirt off." Kane shrugged out of his shirt one-handed as he spoke. "And I'm definitely on the table."

Piper blinked and looked away. Wow. Even after four months of looking at Boone's perfection, Piper was a little stunned at how cut her new client was. Funny how she'd never seen him on the tour before.

"Pants too?" His hands were on his buckle. Oh, he was disrobing. Right here. Piper spun around. She was used to cowboys not being super modest, but this was over the top.

"Ahh, I'll wait outside. There's a blanket you can…um…cover yourself with and um…a robe." She'd not been prepared for him to start stripping in front of her, and Piper scurried out of her own tent.

And straight into Boone.

"What's he doing?" Boone demanded, holding her shoulders and trying to peer into the tent. "He's taking off his clothes? All of them?"

Piper pulled herself together.

"That's not uncommon with massages," she said. She and Boone had talked about this, and he'd always seemed cool with it, if a little dubious. But usually in the rodeo setting, the cowboys had a tendency to not completely disrobe.

"He's married. Has two kids."

Piper stared at Boone.

"Good for him. Why are you being so weird?"

Boone looked a little embarrassed.

"I just… I wasn't expecting him to, you know, strip like right away."

She hadn't either.

"Maybe I should stay here." Boone looked rather imposing already.

"Are you nuts? Privacy is imperative. And I am a professional." Piper pointed at her certificate and kinesiology degree, both of which Boone had had framed for her.

"Nothing Kane Wilder does is private. He's famous. N.O.T.O.R.I.O.U.S," Boone spelled out. "Well at least he was before he got married last year."

"Man crush much?" Piper rolled her eyes at him then she spun her finger in a circle and pointed in the opposite direction.

Boone stayed put.

"You are being ridiculous. You said you'd see me tonight for the picnic so see me tonight."

Boone was still lightly holding her shoulders and he pulled her in roughly and kissed her. Piper shouldn't have been surprised. But she was and her lips parted, which Boone rather passionately took advantage of. Piper almost felt dizzy. First he was cool and distant; now he was in her space and hot.

"I missed you," he breathed against her mouth.

"Hey, Boone, you still trying to get a threesome with me?" Kane poked his head out of the tent. He wore the robe Piper had left out for him. One thing in her favor today.

Boone jumped back, his face immediately washed with pink. Piper was sure she was even redder.

"In your kinky dreams, Wilder," Boone managed.

"Boone was just leaving," Piper stammered.

"Looks like he wanted to be coming." Kane laughed. "Sorry, ma'am, cowboy humor."

"Ha. Ha."

"I like her." He grinned, creased eyes and a huge smile, perfect white teeth, a left dimple and a cleft chin. She suddenly remembered where she'd seen him. In magazine ads. Cologne. High fashion and western wear. And a special type of wicking men's sports briefs that probably left no one noticing the underwear.

"You good to go, baby?" Boone asked her leaning down to look into her eyes and her no doubt flushed face.

"I'm fine," she said. "Really." And at his concerned look she realized that she was. She loved him. And if he didn't love her, it was going to hurt for a long time, but she would find her way. She always had. Knocked down, pop back up. In her own way she was a little like a rodeo cowboy.

"Okay, you staked your claim, cowboy." Kane held up his left hand that had a large gun-metal-colored thick wedding band that was etched with some sort of design. "And I definitely staked mine last year. So back off and let my masseuse do her job. I got finals in a month and I'm tired of driving to Bozeman because the hospital's massage therapist ran off with a married occupational therapist. God. Small towns." Kane shook his head and popped back into her tent.

PIPER PUT HER elbow on Kane's left trapezoid and pushed down, allowing her weight to settle. It took a while, but she felt the muscle release.

"Thanks."

Piper had imagined Kane would be chatty considering the way he'd razzed Boone, but he'd been all business. Telling her where he hurt and what worked best. He knew his body and was in phenomenal shape. She leaned into his right trapezoid and waited for the tension to ease. That one took longer. And by the tension flicking up his back, it hurt. She eased the pressure, letting her eyes drift briefly to the tattoo of the bucking bull scrawled across his upper back.

"Beautiful art," she said softly easing up even more.

"No don't ease up," he said softly. "Harder's good."

Piper dug her elbow in deeper and leaned.

"Thanks, my wife's design."

Finally, Piper felt the release, and she shifted the pressure a little lower.

Kane hissed. "Perfect—don't stop."

Piper looked at his back, mapping out a path that she

thought would be most effective. She'd asked about new injuries, and he was having more trouble with the tendons in his right arm and shoulder. No wonder considering his profession.

"She toured with me one summer too," Kane said. "I hope Boone's not as big of a stupid ass as I was."

Piper tried to let the words wash over her. Keep her professional focus and not let herself slip into her personal space.

"He's young. Probably dumb," Kane added with a laugh. "Been there done that."

Piper bit back the need to defend Boone. She wasn't sure how Boone knew someone so famous.

"But I've heard good things. Boone's solid. Good to his bones."

Piper tried not to let the words get her personally, but she was curious. Kane sounded like he knew Boone, but he was a top-tier bull rider. He didn't work the Montana pro tour. He looked to be close in age. Maybe they grew up together. Temptation. Boone always lived in the moment. She could barely get him to nail down a plan for the day so he rarely talked about the past or the future. Rarely he'd allude vaguely to his family. Here was a chance for her to learn more.

But Boone would tell her if he wanted her to know.

And maybe the bull rider was fishing for more information about their relationship. Piper had grown up around so many secrets—her father's profession was all about a 'need to know basis.' And he'd never talked about her mother or the feelings he had about her walking out on their marriage and toddler, or losing a son he never got to know.

She wondered if her dad had ever held her twin brother, Pace.

She hoped so.

She wished she'd had a photograph. She'd asked once—screwed up her courage when a school assignment required pictures of her family. She'd asked to see a photo of her mother and if there was one of her twin brother. Her father hadn't bothered to answer. He'd just told her to shut the door on her way out.

Piper spread out Kane's right hand and began to work the pressure points in his palm.

"Piper, you are so much more skilled than the masseuse who recently left at the hospital's PT facility. No wonder Boone's upped his game this season."

Piper laughed a little at that. It was true Boone did get special treatment, and she'd learned so much about how cowboys hurt from massaging and icing him and getting him to finally talk to her when he hurt. Cowboys who rode bulls or broncs really got beat up, and even though their bodies healed, their musculature compensated for the stress, and they were phenomenal athletes, it was eventually a losing battle.

She hated to think of Boone hurting. Or of being permanently injured, which she'd learned was a risk.

"I do my best. I'm fully certified, but have focused my studies and practice on athletes." Piper worked his other hand, which didn't have the same tension in the tendons. She handed Kane a bottle of water. "Drink all of this and another one within a couple of hours to help flush out your system. I'm sorry I don't have a longer appointment. I'd like more time with your shoulders, but I have a client due soon. I have time later this afternoon if you want to come back."

"Sounds good." He sat up quickly, and Piper was relieved he pulled the blanket up with him so that his lap was covered. She started backing out of the tent.

"What time?" he asked. "I'd love a go with the reformer. You trained?"

"Four." Piper nodded. "Certified to teach yoga and Pilates and I earned my massage certification in May. I was a dancer for years."

His beautiful but eerie gaze was unnerving. She felt like he could see through her—all of her insecurities that she tried to button up tight.

"You get tired of the tour, Marietta's a great town to build a life in. Plenty of call for your services here—with all the sports enthusiasts who visit and the cowboys who live here, and then the moms." He smiled, and this time it reached his eyes. "You'd have no trouble getting bookings. Witt could get you in tight with the hospital, especially now as they're down a masseuse. Tell Boone not to fuck it up like I did. Took me four years to dig out of that hole. Four years wasted."

Piper didn't know what to say to that. And she had no idea who Witt was, but Kane acted like she should.

Kane reached for his jeans, and Piper turned around to leave to give him the privacy he seemed far too casual about.

"Piper." His voice was rich and deep and seemed like it should belong to a mellower, older man.

"Men make mistakes."

"And women should forgive them?" Piper kept her back to her client. She stared at the slit in her tent. Freedom. She wasn't sure why this conversation was making her tense. Maybe it was the way Kane had dangled the vision of her setting up a practice in Marietta so casually, but he hadn't mentioned Boone. Or maybe it was that he effortlessly belonged, and she didn't.

He came up behind her, and Piper startled. He was fully dressed, and she hadn't even heard him move.

"But forgiveness has to flow both ways," he said easily and tipped his hat. "I learned that the hard way. See you at four. Thanks."

Chapter Seven

BOONE STOOD AT the bar at Grey's. He'd never felt so out of sorts. He wasn't used to analyzing his thoughts, emotions or actions. And he didn't like feeling in the wrong.

Girls at school used to tease him that he should wear a white hat even though he always favored black or a dark tan Stetson his mom had bought him when he'd graduated. Definitely wouldn't qualify for white this weekend.

He needed to come clean.

"Hey, didn't expect to see you here," one of the cowboys Boone knew the best on the tour, Cody, came up behind him and slapped him on the shoulder. "You look like you're studying for an exam. Pick a beer. You always go for a local brew."

Gloomily Boone ordered. Cody laughed and ordered him a whiskey chaser.

"If anyone needs it, you do. What's wrong?"

Normally Boone kept his own counsel. But he liked Cody. He also trusted him even though he had a bad boy rep that he used as a bit of a shield and why not? Touring frayed nerves as well as the body so having some privacy and headspace was essential. Besides, he and Cody had a lot in common. Siblings who were accomplished as hell, while they rode demons for pride and prize and to prove a point to themselves if not to someone else.

"I haven't been honest with Piper," Boone said.

"You? About what?" Cody's astonishment would have been funny, but Boone felt anything but amused. Cody's eyes went wide. "No way."

By Cody's expression, Boone could tell the way his mind was going.

"I'd never." Boone was totally offended.

"Hey." Cody put up his hands. "You'd be the last guy I'd think would…you know…but…" Cody left the word hanging there. "Lots of opportunities."

"Fuck no," Boone objected, tossing back some beer down his throat that suddenly felt Mojave dry.

Flynn O'Connell walked in and he nodded in recognition to Boone and Cody and called over the bartender before making his way toward them.

"Definitely not that. I just haven't told her I grew up in Marietta. I haven't introduced her to my family, and I haven't told my family I've been traveling with her."

He said the words fast and low and they sounded even more stupid out loud.

Cody was a total friend, not pointing out what an idiot he was.

"So how's that going to work exactly?" Cody asked carefully. "That's a pretty low fucking profile you need to keep. Your dad's practically running the show with some of the other rodeo committee members. And don't you usually stay with them at the ranch?"

"Already a sore point," Boone groused.

"Hey." Flynn joined them. "Where's Piper?"

"Stashed away," Cody said.

"Come again?"

Boone took another swig of beer to keep from talking about it, but Flynn's eyes were steely and his face was not that of a man about to give up.

"I don't want to introduce her to my family because then they'll think we're serious. They'll make a big deal of it. She'll think we're serious."

"You sure as hell seem serious. I hardly ever see you apart," Cody pointed out.

"Let's talk about something else."

"Later," Flynn said. "I want to hear how the golden one has a flaw."

"Not that again." Boone hated that nickname. He'd gotten it on the tour his first year because he was always helping everyone out, and one of the veteran bull rider's wives had dubbed him that, and it had unfortunately stuck. Boone felt like people were starting to forget but no, Flynn had to bring it up again.

"This was supposed to be just, you know, fun with Piper."

No reaction. Shane Marvell sauntered in, nodded and went to the bar. Boone took another deep and moody swallow of his beer. "I just feel I need to accomplish more before I…you know…settle down."

"Is Piper pushing for more?" Flynn asked.

"No."

"So what's the sweat?" Flynn shrugged and took a long drag of his beer. "Maybe she's just having fun too?"

"A rodeo cowboy doesn't scream stability to women. We shout temporary, wild ride," Cody said and clinked his beer with Flynn's. "And that's how I like it."

"Have fun and walk away with a smile," Flynn agreed. "That's how I roll."

"Or maybe she'll be the one to walk away with a smile," Cody said. "She's got two college degrees and magic hands. Not like she doesn't have other options."

True.

Piper should walk. He wanted her to walk. Needed her to walk because he didn't seem to have the balls to cut her loose.

"Who's going to walk?" Shane Marvell shoulder-checked Boone. "Hey, stranger. You seem to be avoiding everyone."

Boone ignored him.

"Girl Boone got himself knotted up over," Cody said.

"Why cut her loose now? Wait until the end of the short round." Shane clinked his bottle with Boone's and the beer nearly fell from Boone's hand. "Notice how I'm kindly boosting your confidence by getting you to the short round?" Shane took a long swallow. "Why cause trouble now? Season's winding down, and it's always a grind. Break it off before the break. You'll have a month or so at the ranch to heal, forget, find another woman. My work here is done," Shane said smugly.

Boone had a stupid urge to wipe the laughing smile from Shane's face with his fist even though he knew, absolutely knew Shane was right. It was what he'd planned to do long before he hit Marietta so why the hell was he waiting?

He should tell her tonight. At the picnic. No, that would be awkward. Piper might cry. She'd want privacy. He should do something special for her. A private picnic with just the two of them. Take her someplace beautiful and then… His mind wouldn't allow him to fill in the rest.

He tossed back the whiskey chaser, even though he'd planned to ignore it.

And then Dean Maynard walked into Grey's. All four of them shut up. Tensed. After yesterday at Grey's, Boone knew Dean was ready to pick a fight, and he knew all Boone's triggers. Boone slammed down his glass and turned to face Maynard.

Bring it the fuck on.

Only for once Maynard didn't get in his grill. No. He popped off at Cody. Something about him giving his prize money away to a hot waitress and her sick kid. Boone felt a swell of pride for Cody. He knew his studied indifference and bad boy swagger hid a lot of good, but he also knew no man wanted his business dissected in public, and Cody was more private than many.

One more reason to despise rich, dickhead Dean Maynard.

"Your hair's a gorgeous color," Amanda Wright-Justice, owner of The Wright Salon, said as she worked Piper's hair with a large round brush and blow-dryer.

"I was thinking the same about your hair," Piper said, admiring the long blonde hair that was pulled back in a high retro-style ponytail that tumbled down her back. Everything about Amanda was stylish. And everything about the salon, especially the generous splashes of pink, made Piper happy.

"So you're in town for the rodeo. What do you think of Marietta?"

"I love it. Part of me thinks it's like a movie set so historic and cute, but yet it's so real. I put up some of my cards on a few community boards around town like I've done in a lot of towns, but here the people were so friendly and welcoming, curious about me as a person. It didn't just seem like they were being polite. It's like the town I've always imagined living in."

Amanda smiled. "Careful, you'll end up moving here. Everyone who comes to Marietta seems to fall in love with it.

Even my husband, who arrived in town thinking he'd hate it."

"Why?"

"His father grew up here. But he was a big-city guy." Amanda laughed a little and her face shone with love.

Piper felt a pang of envy. She probably looked like that when she talked about Boone, and she would have thought he felt the same way until yesterday. Thursday, the day of doom, Piper thought, uncharacteristically pessimistic.

She shook off the doubt. The salon was cute. Amanda had given her a glass of sparkling pink water. She and Boone were going to a picnic.

Snap out of it.

"Count me a fan," Piper said, a little surprised she was having such a good time. She often talked to strangers—with all her moves and travels, she had to—but she didn't often feel so relaxed about it.

Amanda looked thoughtful, and again, Piper marveled at how naturally pretty she was. Classically attractive with a slight retro vibe that made her seem like someone Piper would really want to get to know. Become friends with. A little wave of sadness hit her. She wasn't building the life she wanted. She was in a holding pattern. Again. But Boone was everything she'd ever dreamed about. Well, except he seemed restless, looking at some far-off horizon for what, Piper didn't know.

"You said you were putting cards up. I have a notice

board. What are they cards for?"

"I'm a masseuse. I specialize in massage for athletes and injuries, but I'm completely certified. I did specialized training for athletes because I used to be a professional dancer, but…" Piper took the plunge, firmly stating her dream vocally. Next up, she'd act on it. This uncertainty was slowly killing her—hitching her dreams to Boone's wagon was a mistake.

"I'm looking for a town to settle in and build a career as a masseuse. I have a portable massage chair and a portable table and also a professional-grade Pilates reformer. I've been traveling with my boyfriend who's a bull and bareback rider with the Montana pro rodeo circuit. He wrestles steers too. Crazy huh?" But Piper couldn't keep the note of pride out of her voice.

Amanda turned off the blow-dryer and ran her fingers through Piper's thick long hair. It shone under the light.

"Crazy but sexy, I bet."

Piper bit her lip and could see herself blush. So silly. She was an adult now. Building a career. She'd been with Boone a full four months. No more blushing like a young, shy girl, still nervous around boys. Boone was a man and with him as her guide, she'd blown her sexual inexperience to smithereens.

"Crazy sexy."

"No bragging now." Amanda laughed. "I keep it PG in here. Let me freshen up your strawberry sparkling water. And

I have a new shine product I'd like to try on your hair."

Piper relaxed under Amanda's skilled fingers as she massaged her scalp, and fluffed her long hair.

"Bit intimidating giving a masseuse a massage."

Piper laughed. "Not at all. I'm loving it. You have a lovely salon. So welcoming. Great vibe. I feel like I belong, like I could just bring in a coffee and chat."

"That was the goal."

Amanda put a dime-size quantity of clear liquid on her fingers and rubbed them together. Then she took small pieces of Piper's hair and quickly stroked her fingers through.

"What do you think?"

"I love it."

"Next time you're in, I can give you a trim."

"Ends that bad, huh?" Piper winced.

"Not at all. Before you go, let me show you something."

Piper followed her across the small, but stylish salon, admiring all the tasteful touches. It seemed so clever to take an old house and convert it to a business, especially a salon. You were home even when you weren't home. Piper even loved the street it was on. Church Avenue. "Take Me to Church." She loved that song by Hozier. And "My Church" by Maren Morris.

Amanda walked down a short hall, opened a door with a bit of a flourish and stepped into an empty room. Piper followed her in. She looked around and then back at Amanda.

"Just saying. It's here."

Piper eyed the four walls. The light streaming through one window. She looked back at Amanda, an unspoken question in her eyes.

"I've been looking to make this a full-service salon and day spa, but I haven't found the right person. If you're looking for a town to belong and a business to grow, I have the space to rent."

"Oh." Piper looked around the room differently. She walked the perimeter and closed her eyes to feel the space. "Wow."

"Big decision if you're traveling with your cowboy. Montana's a big state, but still not impossible for him to come visit between rodeos. And a big break's coming up. Where does he call home in between?"

Piper startled from her contemplation of the room. "I don't actually know," she said, almost appalled by her ignorance. "I think he's pretty much on his own like I am. We planned to stay together for the summer and then…" Piper shrugged feeling a little stricken.

She was by nature a planner. She'd loved Boone's spontaneity. His easy affection and sense of fun and adventure and the care he took with her. It would be hard to say goodbye. But that had been the plan. And like Amanda said, Montana was a big state, but it was the state where Boone worked, and he said he'd grown up on a ranch in Montana.

Maybe if she settled somewhere like Marietta it didn't

have to be the end for them.

"It's funny," she mused. "From the beginning this town just felt right, like what I was looking for and well…" How to explain the signs she'd seen in a few of her interactions? She didn't want Amanda to think she was a new-age, touchy-feely nut. Even the salon felt right. Amanda and the receptionist, Emily seemed like they could become colleagues, if not friends.

"Think about it," Amanda said and gave Piper her cell number. "I don't have anyone else in mind. I was waiting, feeling like the right person would find me, and I think today they did."

"Thank you," Piper said. "I'll think about it for sure."

"Great. I know it's a big decision, but I am hoping to get a masseuse in here soon, and since you have portable equipment, maybe sometimes you can travel to clients with me. I have a mobile service—an RV in the back."

Piper walked out of the salon feeling elated and terrified, and as she walked back to the rodeo grounds she wasn't sure if she wanted to dance around in excitement or hide and cry. How had something so beautiful turned into something so complicated?

Chapter Eight

BOONE PUT HIS truck in park but kept the engine idling. He looked over at Piper. She smiled.

"You're not really going to blindfold me are you?"

He nodded solemnly.

She felt a little nervous and excited.

"Why?"

"I want to surprise you, and honestly, the thought of blindfolding you excites me."

Piper's breath hitched.

"Does it excite you?" he asked. "Or make you nervous?"

She moistened her upper lip with her tongue. The sun was just beginning to dip lower in the sky, fingers of pink starting to creep out from the horizon.

"Both," she admitted. "But I trust you, Boone."

He winced, but then his face cleared, got intense when he leaned in to her. "I want you to trust me, Piper," he said. "I don't want…I would never…" Boone seemed unable to find the words. "I'd like you to know I would never deliberately let you down. Or…"

"I know."

He slowly drew a bandana from his pocket.

"And you can rely on me, Boone. I want you to be happy," she said in a rush, and she meant it. Even if his happiness came at the expense of hers. Boone was such a good person. She admired him so much—how he always jumped in to help anyone on the tour, even his competitors. And how he always checked in on her—to see if she needed anything, if she were hungry or tired or…anything. After a lifetime of feeling practically invisible, Boone had made her feel vital, and as she stared into his eyes, as the day began to change from golden to gray and pink, she wondered if she'd told him enough how much he meant to her, how much she admired him.

"I am happy." Although he looked a little sad when he said it. "This weekend's been rough. I…I sucked here last year. Wanted to do really well and instead I choked badly. I didn't make the short round on any event, even steer wrestling, and well, I just don't want to go out that route again."

"You won't," Piper said, her smile sunny. "You've been doing well, and you have me as your good luck charm."

He nodded. "I like to keep it low-key before events and I thought the picnic would just be too busy. Plus, I wanted to take you someplace special. So…" He held up the bandana and raised his eyebrows.

Piper leaned in to him and closed her eyes, savoring his scent, the intimacy that seemed to wrap around them so easily again. She closed her eyes. He kissed her tenderly and whispered her name so sweetly like he always did right before he'd enter her when they made love. Then he gently tied the bandana around her.

"Too tight?"

"No."

"Can you see?"

Piper didn't even bother to open her eyes. "No."

"Okay. No peeking."

"Or?"

He laughed. "You want to play, I'll play. I'm going to carry you for a little while to get there so you will be at my mercy. You'll find out what that means if you peek."

Piper nibbled on her lip, but felt happiness wash through her.

It was funny. She'd been looking forward to the barbeque picnic at the park this evening. Amanda had mentioned it and even her client Kane had asked her if she wanted to join his family for it later this evening. Piper had enjoyed meeting so many people native to Marietta, but being alone with Boone had always been special for her.

She was getting her picnic. But Boone was taking her to a special spot. He wanted to be alone with her. That had to mean something, right?

Boone put the truck in gear and they bumped along a very rutted road. She could hear bushes or trees brush along the side of the truck and Boone was driving slowly. The road was rough and twisty, and definitely on an incline.

He stopped the truck.

"Now?"

"Nope. Keep it on, little miss impatient."

She sat in the truck while Boone got something out of the back seat, and then came around to her side. She thought he'd pick her up and carry her the romantic way, but instead he swung her up and over his shoulder.

She yipped in surprise.

Boone laughed. "I need my other hand to carry the picnic basket and blanket."

"I could have walked." Each word felt squeezed out of her as he started walking rather quickly considering he was carrying her and a basket of food.

"Where's the fun in that?"

"Boone, you should probably put me down. You might injure yourself before tomorrow."

He lightly swatted her bottom and she squeaked in surprise.

"What was that for?" She couldn't believe he'd spanked her.

"For doubting my cowboy manliness." He walked a bit further while Piper tried unsuccessfully to stifle her laughter. He stopped. "Is the blindfold still on?"

"Yes."

"Okay. Don't look yet." He gently lowered her to her feet, and then sat her down on what felt like a rock. "It's safe right here, Piper. It's a big granite rock that was sheared off probably eons ago in the Missoula floods. Pieces of these rocks are scattered as far away as Oregon. Imagine the power and fury of that water surging thousands of miles."

Piper felt along the rock with her fingers while she waited. She could hear Boone moving around. Then she heard the pop of a small cork and liquid pouring. Her heart fluttered.

"Did you get champagne?"

He gently untied her blindfold and tucked it in his back pocket while she blinked at him.

He handed her a glass of sparkling wine. "Just a split since I'm riding tomorrow and you don't drink much. You're supposed to be looking at the view," he said quietly.

"I am," Piper said barely able to swallow as emotion swamped her.

"The other view." He smiled.

Boone settled near her on the rock and she looked out over gently rolling hills, with a narrow ribbon of river flowing through it.

"You've showed me so many beautiful places, Boone," Piper said softly thinking of all the national parks they'd visited in Montana and Utah. All the mountains they'd hiked in Colorado. "We aren't trespassing are we?"

Boone hesitated. He looked pensive as he stared across the valley. "Not exactly. It's been Crawford County land forever, but I heard it's going up for auction soon. Too soon," she thought she heard him mutter.

"Thank you for sharing your favorite view with me."

He nodded. Released a long breath much like a pricked balloon.

"Boone?"

He startled almost as if he'd forgotten she was there.

"Sorry, Piper." He took her hand. She waited. Felt like she was holding her breath. "You warm enough? Gets cold when the sun goes down."

"I'm fine. Boone, what is it?" She'd already put on a sweater.

"Let's just enjoy the view a little bit." Boone slipped his arm around her shoulder and they sat quietly, watching the sun sink and the pink and gray claim the blue of the sky. Piper's heart raced. Boone seemed like he wanted to say something, and part of her wanted to insist he tell her, but another, larger, cowardly part insisted she remain silent.

His thumb sketched circles on her back, and Piper relaxed in to him. She was torn. She wanted to discuss what she'd learned today—about the potential to open a massage studio in Amanda Wright's Salon, and she wanted to discuss their future—if they had one. But as she turned the words over and over in her head, she could feel her courage bleed out. The view was beautiful. Boone had packed a picnic. He wanted to be alone with her. If this was one of her last memories with him, she wanted to enjoy it, not spoil the moment by overanalyzing and planning out every move. She admired Boone's spontaneity, and should try it on sometimes.

But no. She knew that wouldn't ultimately work for her. She had to make decisions. And she needed to know where she stood with him. She sucked in a breath.

"I brought food," Boone said. "You want me to make you up a plate?"

"Sure." He'd gone to so much trouble. And he had an active life. He must be hungry.

She settled on the blanket across front him, their knees bumping.

"Do you like Marietta?"

"Love it," he said as he scooped some rice on her plate, cucumber and tomato salad, chickpeas and roasted peppers and a chicken skewer.

Piper laughed. "No wonder you wanted to go off by ourselves—this is not typical cowboy fare."

Boone handed her the plate along with a fork. He grinned.

"It's true you've introduced me to some pretty unMontana things. Other competitors on the tour are beginning to notice. I might lose my tour card."

"I haven't unmanned you, cowboy," she teased. "I've upped your game."

"You have, Piper." He smiled, and Piper caught her breath.

He was so physically perfect, effortlessly handsome in a

way that always made him seem a little unreal, and out of reach. But it was his innate goodness and the way he took care of her that always undid her. And how he would try new things to please her. So maybe she should help him now—help him to tell her what was bothering him.

"We've been traveling together for four months, Boone," Piper said softly, wanting to somehow jump-start the conversation about the future without getting heavy.

He nodded, his face not closing off entirely, but he seemed to turn inward. His blue eyes met hers and held. Then he leaned forward and kissed her. Her lips immediately went pliant under his, and she quickly put her plate off to the side so she could hold on to him.

"Behave now," he said softly breaking off the kiss, his breathing elevated as he rested his forehead against hers. "I could kiss you forever, Piper. Never get tired of it."

"Me too," she breathlessly agreed.

"But we always take it to the next level pretty quick and I'm trying to be a gentleman tonight."

"You're always on your best behavior," Piper defended.

He laughed a little ruefully and filled his plate. "I'm pretty sure your father, the colonel, wouldn't agree."

Piper waved her hand, dismissing her father. He hadn't agreed on anything she could remember, and she doubted he cared or thought about her much.

"What's been the biggest change having me on tour with you?" Piper impulsively asked when he filled a plate for himself—more chicken and no chickpeas.

He picked up his chicken kabob, his eyes out the horizon, as the sun slipped lower. "Everything is better," he said, thrilling her.

"But you've done the rodeo since you were eighteen. You must have had other girlfriends travel with you."

Boone shook his head. "I told you I never did before. I mean I…you know…met up with girls over the weekends and had drinks and danced and sometimes more if they wanted." He seemed uncomfortable with the conversation.

"Why me?"

Boone ate the chicken straight off the stick. He shrugged a little.

"Don't you wonder why we hit it off so fast?"

"We just did." He picked up another kabob.

"But you'd never done that before, met a woman and clicked instantly and invited her to travel with you for a few weeks or a month or longer?"

Boone shrugged. "Too distracting. Too irritating."

"You never get short with me, Boone. I can't imagine you ever being so solitary. Why did you invite me after only two days of knowing each other?"

"I didn't really analyze it, Piper. It just sounded fun and you were game and it's been a good ride." He seemed ready to climb out of his skin. "Why did you come?"

She stared into his face, wondering if she should tell him—if she could explain it to him in a way he'd understand without scaring him to death.

"It sounded like an adventure. And very glamorous."

He laughed. "Yeah, all the dust and manure and animal smells and taping up my body. And going on extra ice runs after I compete. Totally glamorous."

"It was you, Boone," Piper said. "You. The way you looked at me and smiled at me. It made me feel alive and connected in a way I never had before," she admitted in a broken whisper.

He met her gaze and held it, and Piper felt totally exposed. She was on a ledge. She could jump or walk it back.

"But then it was taping up your bruises. And I always did have a kinky thing for ice," she said taking a giant metaphorical step backward to safety.

"Ice, huh? I did pack some ice to keep your kale salad cool."

"Careful, cowboy, those are serious seduction words."

Piper picked up a chickpea from off her plate. "Try it," she said. "I dare you."

He made a face. "What will you give me?"

"Probably another one because you'll ask so nicely."

He took the chickpea from her fingers swallowed it, likely without tasting it, but sucked her finger deep into his mouth. His tongue lightly stroking it. Piper felt her entire body go soft and damp. "Please, Piper. Pretty please. Can I have another…" He let the sentence stretch, his smile wicked.

"Chickpea?"

He moved his plate off his lap.

"No," he said softly, his voice as deep and dark as sin. "That's not the word I was thinking of. Unless—" he drew out the S sound "—you let me put the chickpea someplace more interesting."

"I dare you, cowboy."

She was already unsnapping his shirt, and tugging it out of his jeans and off his shoulders, her hands greedy and intent.

He smiled. "Careful, I might take you up on that."

"Go ahead. I double dare you," Piper said, her hands busy. She pushed on his chest, and he allowed himself to be forced back on the blanket.

"Damn, girl, I love how you're always as eager as me, but I'm getting cheated. You have on all your clothes. Again." Still, he let her undress him, toeing off his boots. Her hand was at his buckle, snaking the leather through his belt loops.

But when he reached for her, she was already straddling him and taking the belt and looping it around his hands. "Jesus, Piper." His eyes flared with both surprise and arousal.

"Seems only fair. You blindfolded me. And spanked me."

"That was not a spanking. Not even close."

"Still, take your punishment." Piper looped the belt around his wrists. It wasn't effective but Boone played along. She liked him like that, willing to play. Stretched out for her. His chest bare, his arms above his head, and his arousal obvious and pressing against his jeans for release. It gave her a sense of control she'd felt she'd lost since yesterday. She straddled his thighs and caught the fabric around the first button of his Levi's with her teeth and tugged.

A groan ripped from Boone's throat and his hips jerked upward. Piper licked at the opening and then tugged open another button.

"Be still," she said as he writhed under her.

"I want to…"

"This is about what I want tonight," Piper interrupted and she exhaled warm air along his skin.

"Oh, God," Boone breathed out.

It still amazed Piper the power she had over him sexually. And he over her. He'd turn the tables in a second. Boone might be sweet and gentle, but he was dominant in bed and she loved that side of him—the side where he'd catch fire so quickly and have to have her. *Have* to.

But she wanted to control this a little because she had a surprise for him. She undid another button and lapped at the opening with her tongue as her hands pulled his jeans over his hips and down his legs where he kicked them off. Piper cupped his balls, rolling them gently when she took him into her mouth. She loved the way he tasted and felt—silky but oh so hard.

Boone gave up the pretense of handing over control. He tossed the belt somewhere and his hands were buried in her hair while he hoarsely whispered encouragement. Piper loved this. Loved bringing Boone pleasure. She liked it even more than when he did this to her. She never had any idea sex could be so intimate, that she could feel like she was part of another person so entirely, feel like she was deep in their skin and blood and wrapped around their bones, and he inside her.

She swirled her tongue around his leaking tip, savoring his salty masculine essence. Torn, she wanted to keep going, but she wanted to ride him as the sun set and twilight took over. She wanted to lie with him under the stars.

"You look so beautiful Piper but way overdressed."

She kept her hand wrapped around his erection and gently pumped it. She smiled at him, feeling mysterious, playful and sexy in a way she hadn't before. Usually she let Boone take the lead, but she had so many questions and worries and emotions rattling around her head right now that she felt more assertive—ready to bust out and take charge.

"I thought you liked this dress." She kissed her way up his abdomen.

"I'd like it better off."

"I can still take care of you, Boone. Give you what you want."

Piper raised herself up a little and guided him to her slick heat. She teased him along her seam.

"Piper, you weren't wearing underwear this whole time? Damn, I wouldn't have made it out of the trailer if I'd known that."

Piper kept herself just out of reach, loving having control. "Then we would have missed the beautiful scenery."

"All I see are stars. Get up here. I want to taste you. Make you scream."

Not like he gave her much choice. He gripped her hips and his mouth was on her even as her dress settled over him.

Piper could barely remain upright as his tongue immediately teased her swollen clit with moist heat. She cried out as he stroked her close to a climax and then backed off.

"Keep your dress on," he demanded, "but let the straps fall down, touch your breasts. You're not wearing a bra are you? Get rid of the bra, baby."

It felt decadent and absolutely perfect to have Boone under her, his mouth working magic while she cupped her breasts, and imagined it was his hands on her, his fingers working her nipples, making them peak and ache.

Boone kissed and nipped her inner thighs while his thumb stroked her and two of his fingers dipped deep into her heat. He brought her to the brink again, only this time he tipped her over fast, and even as her body started to spasm, Boone caught her and shifted her weight back so that he was over her.

He hesitated. "Piper, I didn't bring…"

"It's okay," she interrupted desperate to have him inside her. Skin to skin. Nothing between them. "You're safe."

"We're safe," he corrected. "Piper, I need to take care of you," he said urgently.

"Then do it." She wrapped her legs around his narrow hips and tilted her pelvis, catching him, her hands clasping his bare ass, and he sank into her with a groan, and Piper hissed as her muscles clenched around him. And then Boone was inside of her, hot and hard and moving in long smooth strokes through her orgasm. He splayed one hand across her ass cheek to keep the pressure where she was most sensitive and Piper felt herself fly into another orgasm even as Boone kept moving inside of her.

She clung to him, trying to not rake her nails down his back even though she kept them trimmed short for work. She never wanted it to end, never. She felt him tense and anticipating his climax she clenched her muscles and savored his shout, and the splash of his hot seed bathing her core.

Piper held him to her, soaked in the after quakes, and their ragged breathing. Even if she never could be with Boone again, she wanted to remember this moment, nothing separating them. Feeling him fly apart inside of her. But he'd never not worn a condom with her. That had to mean something, right? She tried to stamp down on her stupid, soaring heart.

"I'm too heavy," he murmured, trying to lift himself off her.

"You're perfect. This is perfect." She sighed.

He slipped her dress down to her waist so they were bare skin to bare skin.

He sighed. "Better."

"The best," Piper whispered. She couldn't imagine her life without him in it, but she knew she was going to have to ask him questions. Just not now. But soon. "Perfect."

"I WISH YOU had one of those old-fashioned trucks with the long seat so I could sit closer to you," Piper said after they'd packed up everything and were heading back to the trailer.

It was dusk and cool, but Piper still had the window open so she could feel the coming night. She had on Boone's denim jacket. Usually he had the radio on, but not tonight. His hand was splayed across her thigh. Piper tried to hold on to the intimacy from earlier but it leached away like the light.

"It's September," Piper said.

As if neither of them knew that.

"Yeah." Boone's voice was a little more cautious now—like he got when she brought up anything too personal, Piper realized with a pang.

Like he wanted to keep her at arm's length even as he held her close.

"We had talked about me touring with you for the summer." Piper took the plunge. And held her breath.

"Yeah."

Not much to work with.

"What are we doing, Boone?"

He didn't answer for a long time. He turned on the truck's headlights as he maneuvered down the rutted drive back to a wider gravel road.

"Boone?"

He shrugged, and his face pinched a little. "I don't really analyze things except my rodeo rides and stats," Boone finally said. "Never been a planner."

"What's that supposed to mean?"

"You just rocked my world back there, Piper. Fireworks every time with you. Why can't we leave it at that?"

Why couldn't she?

"Because I want more," she finally said.

The silence in the truck was painful. Boone turned onto a narrow paved road.

"More?" he finally asked, but didn't look at her.

"Yeah. I think about the future. My future. What I want, and I want to know what you want."

Boone's hand left her thigh, and she immediately missed his touch. He pushed his hat back and then forward again, always a sign he was thinking and not really liking where his mind or the conversation was going. He put both hands on the wheel.

Part of Piper wished she'd left it, but another part, a bigger part, pushed on.

"I know we talked only about the summer, but I don't think it works like that—an arbitrary end date. Tonight with the picnic and making love didn't feel like we're through, but it's September."

"The tour runs through mid-October," Boone said

quickly, his shoulders sagging a little in what looked like relief.

Piper watched him. His eyes looked tight. No ready smile for her. No hand in her hair or finger brushing along her cheek.

"And then what?" She continued on because clearly he wasn't going to do any of the work for her. "What do you do after the tour? I know the finals are in January. But what do you do November and December? February through early May."

"Mainly I help out at my family's ranch," Boone said cautiously. "My dad's raised cattle as did his dad and his dad before him and on and on. And my mom has bred horses—cutting horses for the rodeo. But my dad wants to expand the business—move into breeding bucking broncs and bulls for the rodeos. Become a rodeo stock contractor."

That sounded good to Piper. Grounded. Some travel. Still having involvement in the rodeo, the life he loved. And it was the first concrete mention of his family. So he did have a relationship with them. Her heart leapt in hope.

"But?"

"Why's there got to be a but?" Boone reached behind him into the cooler and pulled out two bottles of water. He handed one to Piper and uncapped his with his teeth, spit out the cap and took a long swallow.

Piper watched his throat work, and even though she felt like her heart was breaking, she couldn't help but admire how handsome he was. And marvel at how deeply she'd come to love him. She didn't want to hurt. And she didn't want to hurt him, but Piper was tired of drifting with the current.

She needed to put her feet down. Push for what she wanted.

"I sense a but. Don't you enjoy helping your family on the ranch?"

"What? No." He paused. "I love it." The words seemed dragged from his soul thrashing and kicking.

"So…what? You always seem reluctant to talk about your family or your ranch. And you didn't really mention them this summer. Visit them." She had to say it. Ranches took a lot of work.

Boone shrugged. Took another swallow of water and wiped off his mouth with his sleeve. "It's not that, Piper. I love my family. I love the ranch. It's just that it's…it's theirs."

She turned that over in her mind. "You don't feel like you belong?" she asked cautiously finally feeling he was giving her something to work with.

"I belong too well." He smiled without humor. "I'm my father's youngest son. Everyone knows me in connection to my parents and my siblings. Everything I have is from my father's hard work. It's been his family's ranch for generations, but his dad struggled, nearly lost it. My dad rescued the ranch with all of his rodeo earnings. All his hard-earned money. He met my mom on the tour, married her and brought her home and together they built up the ranch. They're still building up the ranch but it's theirs. In their image. Sure they want me to come home and work it with them, because I'm their son."

"And you don't want to be a rancher?"

He stared intensely out the window. She didn't think he would answer.

"Part of me wants that. I do. I love the land and the life. Being outdoors all day allows me to breathe. But it's theirs. I haven't made my own mark. I'm not bringing anything to the ranch but my name."

Piper stroked his arm down to his hand on the steering wheel and placed hers over his as he drove. She knew how proud Boone was. How independent, so she understood his feelings a little, but being part of a family legacy seemed like heaven, a no-brainer, a place to belong and to build dreams.

"Have you told them that?"

He looked startled. "No. They're all about family. The ranch and building a family legacy. Family is everything. If you're family, you have a place. They wouldn't understand."

He blew out a gust of air. "You're good with words, Piper. You put everyone at ease. Explain things well. I'm more action. My thinking gets scrambled."

"You're doing just fine," she assured him. "It's important to try. And if it takes a few times, then people just have to be patient."

Piper hated that she'd left it this long. She should have been trying to get Boone to open up more much earlier. Learn to trust her. Instead she'd let him dictate so much of the relationship.

"Is that why you work so hard on the rodeo? To make your own mark? To earn enough to buy your own property?"

"I don't know about that." Boone looked embarrassed. "My dad was fearless and one of the best bareback riders on the circuit. Top bull rider too. My stats aren't anywhere near his. My earnings aren't even comparatively close. By my age my dad was married, and my mom was expecting my brother Rohan. He was one year from retirement. He was a legend. I'm just good. Dumb enough to keep doing it."

Piper bit back the instant denials and replies that tangled on her tongue and instead let herself think. She thought of Boone as so confident. She never imagined he was harboring self-doubt.

"When do you see yourself retiring?"

"Haven't given it much thought."

"And what would you like to do after the rodeo? You must have given that some thought."

"Not really. Just focus rodeo to rodeo."

Piper tried not to look too astonished. She thought out everything. Over and over. Planned. Anticipated. Calculated.

Boone had been her one impulse.

Sure she'd made mistakes, but she'd cut her losses and moved on. Boone just seemed adrift.

"But if you don't want to work on your parents' ranch…surely you must have some idea of what you want to do? School or…"

He shook his head no. "I didn't do well in school. Had trouble sitting still and listening that long. And something was wrong. I didn't learn to read for a long time. My parents spent a fortune on tutors."

"There's lots of other things you could do."

"I love ranching," Boone said. "What about you? What do you want?"

"I want a home," Piper said. And it was like a cork popped. "I want a town that's small but friendly, and where I know people and they know me, and I want a job that I like where I feel like I can make a difference." She started listing her wants on her fingers.

"That's why I chose massage. It's technical and in a health care field but flexible, and I can work for myself anywhere but also in a clinical or spa setting. I can help people feel good and teach them about healthier lifestyles and caring for themselves. But I want more. I want to go to a coffee shop where I know the barista and the owner. I want to know their kids. I want them to know my order. And I want a go-to restaurant where I have a favorite dish and I can chat with the wait staff and owners. I want friends and a family and a man who loves me and who I love back just as fiercely."

Boone stared at her, his eyes huge. Then he forcefully

looked back at the road.

"That sounds good, Piper." He sounded like he was choking. He drained his water.

He drove longer, the road unfurling behind them, and Piper felt like they were driving into the night. Into the dark.

But I'll find the light again.

She had to be prepared for this. Boone was worth the risk, but how could they have a future when he couldn't even see past tomorrow? Could she help him? Did it just take time? Patience?

"Sounds real good. You deserve it. All of it. Really." He sounded like he was trying to convince himself.

Piper saw the silhouette of the grandstand, and was surprised at how quickly they'd gotten back to town using a different route. He drove the truck carefully thorough the field toward his trailer. Many more trailers and some tents were set up. Some cowboys looked to be camping out in their trucks, and there were some small trailers, lights on, generators humming.

Boone stopped the car and played with his keys, then he turned toward her.

"I want all of that for you. I know what it means to you. You told me how lonely you felt growing up. You told me your mother left when you were a toddler and that you were never close to your dad." He looked pained for her. "I'm sorry, Piper, I'm just not there yet. I wish I could be for you, but I have to be my own man first before I can be someone else's man—someone they can love and depend on through thick and thin."

Piper felt her eyes prick but she forced back the tears and searched his dear features. Boone didn't see himself at all how she saw him. He was that man.

She brought his hand to her cheek. Kissed his palm and closed his fingers one by one. He pressed his hand against his chest. It was a sweet gesture. He'd done it with her before, showing her he held her heart, that he'd take care of it even though he'd never used the words.

"All of those things will come to you, Piper. I know they will."

"But how can you know it's not you and that you're not ready if you don't know what it is you want, what you're searching for?"

He leaned forward and kissed her mouth, so softly and sweetly that a couple of traitorous tears splashed his knuckle. He tasted them.

"Don't cry, baby. Be happy. We have now. That may be all we ever get and it's good. Better than good."

She nodded. It was true. She'd been around the rodeo long enough to know that one misstep could spell disaster. And from her own life one biological or genetic fluke could spell life for one baby, but death for another. And that not all marriages survived loss. And along with illness, accidents and betrayal, life was a crapshoot, and she couldn't control the roll of the dice any more than Boone could.

But she wanted to try with him.

"Let's get you in bed. I'll clean up and then check on Sundance before I join you."

"I'll clean up. You have an early start tomorrow."

Boone pressed his thumb into her bottom lip and looked at her, his expression unusually pensive. "I'll take care of everything," he said helping her to slide out of the truck. He handed her his keys. "It will give me a chance to clear my head for tomorrow."

Piper nodded and went into the trailer and to bed alone.

Chapter Nine

SATURDAY MORNING, PIPER finished with a client, taking her time even though she sensed she was running late. While she loved that her traveling business was growing a little each weekend and the cowboys always tipped great, she worried she'd miss one of Boone's events. The bareback competition always kicked off the rodeo lineups, so who needed caffeine to get the day going?

Piper shrugged out of her white wrap cotton coat that she felt made her look more professional and hung it up, and she quickly stripped the sheet on the bed and wiped down her massage chair and table and then remade the table with fresh linens. That was the hardest thing about being a traveling masseuse—the laundry. Boone never complained, but having to stop for a few hours to wash the bedding before heading out of or into the next town felt like a ginormous bore to her, and it was for her business. But Boone happily joined her at the laundry each time, and then he'd keep her company often, maintaining his ropes while they waited.

She used her wipes to clean her hands as well, and then checked her watch. Definitely late. Boone had drawn a bronc named Hellfire. His bull this afternoon was Deviant Devil. Nothing scary about those names. Piper tried to shrug off her worry.

She was still processing last night. He'd basically told her he wasn't ready for commitment, but wanted them to stay together until October. What would another month change? Would Amanda still have the massage room available? Should she put a deposit down or pay a month's rent to hold it? The questions had turned round and around in her head as she'd tried to sleep.

She could tell she meant more to Boone than just fun and good sex. She knew she did. She could tell it with everything he did even if he seemed to be shutting her out this weekend. When he'd come into the trailer about an hour later last night, he'd been quiet. He'd taken a shower and slipped into bed while Piper pretended to sleep. He'd gently kissed her and curled his body around hers, and Piper had finally relaxed enough to doze off.

This morning, everything had seemed normal between them and Piper had played along, not wanting him distracted for today. She'd fixed him a light, nutritious breakfast and kissed him goodbye saying she'd see him later—like he wasn't heading off into danger.

She hurried to the grandstand just as she heard the announcer call out the rider before Boone. She didn't have time to climb up and find a seat so instead she tucked down low next to a few children and smiled at them, feeling a little like a conspirator.

Slide of metal and out thrashed the horse. Up and down and a spin and the rider was off before the five-second mark. Piper bit back a cry of worry, but the cowboy popped up and ruefully watched the horse race off, tossing its head a little arrogantly as if to say 'I dealt with that arrogant idiot.'

And Boone was next. Piper saw him up on top of the chute talking to a man she'd seen him with several times yesterday—older and dark, but with a wide smile and dimples. He looked like he was laughing, but Boone looked serious, intent. He dropped down onto the back of the restless bronc, and Piper felt her heart kick up a notch.

It was crazy what Boone did. And exciting. Sometimes, Boone would give the nod right away to release the bronc. Other times it took a spell, which always ratcheted up the tension. Today, Piper ticked off the seconds in her head. Boone was clearly working on his grip or trying to get balanced. She so wanted him to have a good ride.

"Let's give a warm welcome to our hometown cowboy—Boone Telford, everyone," the announcer called out.

Piper had been clasping her hands, praying, but she jerked her head up to look toward the announcer. She must have misheard. "Y'all know Boone. He's been a fixture on the Montana rodeo scene since he was a little tow-head hanging on for dear life on his first mutton bust." A lot of people were standing and cheering. Piper saw a few signs.

"We've seen Boone ride and rope since he was in the junior rodeo circuit. Having his best year yet. So let's give him a proper Marietta shout-out."

No way.

Impossible.

It was a mistake.

Boone would have told her he was from Marietta.

He wouldn't have let her read all about the town on the website like that.

He wouldn't have let her go on and on about the town and how cute it was, and how she felt at home here when he was the one who was home.

The announcer read a few stats, even told a joke or two while Piper stared numbly at a beautiful blonde woman and a younger version of her holding up a sign with a picture of Boone. Piper recognized the young woman she'd seen briefly yesterday as the singer of "America the Beautiful" from the grand reopening. They were in the family section with another couple and a tween girl who had another Boone sign up.

Piper had never sat in the family section.

And she hadn't been invited today to sit with his real family.

The chute opened and Boone, nearly horizontal to the bronc, burst out. His left hand was stretched out high as the bronc bucked, swinging its body sideways before slamming up and down. Boone kept his body loose and nimble anticipating the moves before they happened, but it still astonished Piper how Boone held on. How any of them held on to such a wicked force of physics.

She laughed a guttural 'ha' as if to see if she could still speak.

She couldn't believe how stupid she'd been. Naïve.

Great sex wasn't love.

And Boone definitely didn't love her. And another month wouldn't make a difference.

Eight seconds. The audience roared their approval. Piper clutched the fence like she was going to fall and stared, still in total shock. The cheers, the dirt, the smell of sawdust, hotdogs and popcorn and animal all just floated around in some other world she wasn't a part of.

She'd been lying to herself as clearly as Boone had been lying. Well he hadn't lied, she admitted. He just hadn't told her the truth or let her in. He hadn't offered her more. And he hadn't said he loved her. So really the only true deception was the one once again she was practicing on herself—if she tried hard enough, if she were pretty enough, smart enough, helpful enough, cheerful enough—someone would love her.

Only Boone didn't.

Boone was pulled safely off the bronc and now stood tall and proud on the arena floor. He tipped his hat to the crowd—probably looking for his family and their all-important approval.

She walked away from the place where she knew she didn't belong.

WHERE WAS PIPER?

Boone looked toward the section where she'd usually sat in every arena—to the left near an exit. She was so slim it was always easy for her to squeeze herself into a seat. She never missed any of his rides. He didn't see her anywhere. He saw his mom and sister Riley, and sister-in-law Miranda and brother, Witt and Petal cheering. His dad had been with him at the chute. But no Piper.

He hopped over the fence to the backstage area. He already had Sundance ready because he had a quick change-out for the next event: steer wrestling. He'd been a late draw for the bronc and early for the steer wrestling. But he felt edgy and couldn't settle without seeing Piper. She always watched his events. Always. And after their talk last night, he felt like they were more settled. They'd cleared the air. Mostly.

Instead his dad walked toward him.

"Textbook. Ride of beauty," his dad enthused and slapped him on the back. "Eighty-five definitely puts you high on the list for the short event. Well done."

"Thanks," Boone said. When he'd been growing up he'd always counted on praise and advice from his dad—lapped it up like a plant needing water. But not now.

"Sorry, I'll be right back."

"Wait. What? You can't walk out," his dad said. "You're in the next event. You have to check in or they'll scratch your ass."

"I know. I will."

Once he found Piper.

Boone nearly crashed into Cody who sauntered toward him, scrolling through his phone.

"Sorry," Boone muttered, aware his dad was still staring. "Wasn't paying attention," he muttered the obvious. "You see Piper?" he asked, keeping his voice low.

"She headed out just as your ride ended and chest beating started." Cody didn't look up.

"Where?"

Cody blew out a breath and looked Boone dead in the eye. "Leave it," he advised. "Your head's been all over the place since yesterday, and you got another event. Play kiss and make up later."

"Make up?" Boone repeated. They'd talked it out last night. Well, not the Marietta and family part.

And then it hit him. He'd been so focused in on his ride, in his zone, that he hadn't heart much of anything. Not even his dad's terse directions when he saw how jacked the bronc was. But his name would have been announced and each rodeo always did a little extra for their hometown cowboys.

Shit.

"Which direction? Her tent?"

Cody shook his head. Indecision warred on his face.

"Tell me," he said tersely.

"Your funeral," Cody said. "She headed toward the park or maybe downtown. She looked like she was trying to hold it together." Cody shrugged, but his eyes held sympathy. "She was crying."

Boone hopped a fence and then another. His number from the bronc event was still pinned to his shirt. He took off at a run.

He saw her almost immediately as she hadn't gone very far. She was leaning against the Bozeman news station van that was parked toward the dressing room entrance to better take advantage of the competitors coming and going. Piper was bent over, arms wrapped around her stomach.

"Piper," he called out, only his voice sounded winded. He continued to close the space between them fast. "Piper," he tried again louder and this time she heard him.

She stood up. Her eyes sparkled with tears, but she also looked pissed. Really, really pissed.

"I can't believe you didn't tell me you grew up here!" She balled her fists and walked toward him. "What kind of stupid game are you playing?"

"I…"

"What reason could you possibly have for not telling me?" She was in his face now, and Boone stared down at her feeling more at a loss for words than he ever had. Piper was more hurt than angry.

Anger he could deal with. Maybe. The few times he'd screwed up as a kid, his parents had been firm, but never yellers. And Boone didn't usually piss people off. He was the peacemaker. But when Piper's voice cracked and her eyes welled, her hurt made him feel like a cooler of ice water had been dumped on him. His body felt frozen. His brain useless.

"I told you all the places I grew up. How I grew. Moving every year or two. Sometimes every six months."

"I know."

"Why was growing up in Marietta a secret? Why did you feel like you had to keep your family a secret from me?"

Shit.

"I told you about my father. How he's now a colonel. How we were never close. How the Army is his life. I told you about my twin brother who died inside my mother. I told you how my mother left me and my father when I was two. She could never get over losing a baby so she left me behind too to forget both of us. I told you I feel like subconsciously my father blames me for my twin's death—how he never got the son he wanted because of me. I told you all of it." She had tears coursing down her cheeks and she dashed them away.

"It's not like I was one of your weekend hookups and yes, I heard about those from a lot of the other cowboys trying to warn me early on."

Boone jerked like she'd shot him, and in a way he wished

she had.

"We've been together for four months, Boone. I deserve better than to be treated like a woman you just picked up for the night."

Where to start with all of that? So many words. He just wanted to soothe her, but when he moved toward her, Piper backed away.

"Piper, I'm sorry," he tried, and it was such a dumb beginning, even he winced in shame. "I didn't mean to hurt you. Not introducing you to my family...I didn't want..." He grasped for words. He just wasn't used to upsetting anyone. He'd often stepped into tense situations and defused the tension. But he had no idea what to say or what to do to make this right.

And this was very public. Cowboys he rode with, competed against for the past few years were definitely stopping and staring before they'd shuffle off a little and pretend to ignore him and Piper.

"Your family?" Her voice cracked. "You didn't want me to meet your family?"

"It's not what you're thinking," he said hastily.

Shit. Shit. Shit.

"I'm pretty sure it is." She backed away from him. Her eyes had gone squinty. "So I'm good enough to hang out with and...and...fuck for a few months but not meet your parents for lunch or something."

Boone winced at the crudity of her language. He'd never

heard Piper swear. He tried to watch his language around her.

"Jesus, that's not it at all. Christ, Piper." He looked around. Everyone in their vicinity—cowboys, stock hands—all were studiously busy and not looking at him. "Can we go somewhere more private?" he spit out between his teeth. He didn't want anyone thinking that about Piper, especially Piper.

And damn this whole disaster would get back to his father and mother and likely the whole town by this afternoon. His own fault totally. He'd let everything spiral out of control because he hadn't wanted to lose her. Or hurt her. And now he'd done both.

Selfish, he condemned himself, tasting the word like scorched earth in his mouth.

He tried to take her hand, but she jerked it away.

"Please, Piper." He lowered his voice. "Let me explain."

"No." Her voice held a sob, and she was shaking. "You should have told me when we were driving down the mountain into the town at the latest."

"I know. I'm sorry," he said miserably.

She just stared at him like he was a stranger.

"That's not good enough," Piper said, drawing herself up straight. "You're better than that, and I deserve so much better."

"I know. You do. I tried to tell you last night."

"Oh, with the champagne? And the view? And the 'leave

your dress on and touch yourself while I…'"

"Jesus, Piper." He winced and looked around. "I didn't mean for it to go this far. Not like this." His voice sounded like it was leaching out of his bones.

"That's right. You don't like to plan things out. Just go with the flow."

"Boone, what the hell?" Cody appeared at the door leading into the dressing room, some ten yards away. "Your event's next. You're tenth draw. Get your ass ready. Kissy later. Hey, Piper."

"Coming." Boone didn't break eye contact with Piper. "Piper, please. It's not what you think. I know it was stupid. Totally stupid, but it's all on me, not you."

She took another step back. Away from him. Boone closed the distance, but she held out her hand, palm out.

"That tired breakup phrase. It's me. Not you. Fine. You don't want to say it or do it, I will. We're through. You can have your hometown and your family and your friends all to yourself. Knock yourself out."

"Boone." Cody was insistent, and Boone saw his father striding toward him.

"Busy."

"Damn, Boone. You going to scratch? You need to check in. This is always your top event." Cody took a few steps toward him, expression incredulous.

Boone waved him away.

"Go," Piper said and dashed away the last of her tears.

"Not like this. We have to talk this out."

"Nothing more to say, Boone, don't sweat it," she said. "You're still the golden one, untarnished. You offered me a summer and adventure. You delivered. It's September. Go wrestle a steer. Make your hometown proud. Have dinner with your family."

She spun away.

"Piper." He hurried after her. She shook him off.

"Don't follow me. Don't touch me," she hissed, and he drew back from her as if she'd burned him. "Go. Leave. I need to think, and I want to be alone."

"I can't leave you like this."

"I'm fine. I'm good at taking care of myself. I've had my whole life to practice."

Everything she said made him feel worse.

"Piper, please, can we talk later?" he asked.

"I don't know what to say to you, Boone. Just go. Stop drawing this out. Do your event. Make your mark. Just go."

"That's what you want?"

She crossed her arms tightly across her chest and drew an imaginary line in the withered brown grass of the field. "What *I* want?" she repeated hollowly. "I'm so far away from what I want I can't even see it anymore. But I need you to go. Now."

"YOU ARE OVER-REACTING," she told herself fiercely.

"Absolutely over-reacting. This was a summer fling. Nothing more."

She forced herself to walk fast away from the rodeo grounds and the arena. If she said it enough she'd start to believe it.

"I will be strong," she vowed, wishing like she had so many times that she had her brother beside her, her twin, that fate had let him live and thrive and carve out a life with her in it. "Ufffff!" Blinded by her tears, Piper smacked into someone.

"For being so small you pack a whack. Oh hey, bad day huh?"

Piper blinked and found herself staring into the face of one of the most beautiful women she'd ever seen. Her expression went from amusement to concern. "Let me guess: fight with the boyfriend?"

Normally Piper was more reticent. But she was trying to change, right? Remake her life. Belong somewhere? And she felt so scraped raw inside, she didn't even recognize herself.

She nodded. More miserable than before.

"Cowboy?"

"Not a shocker there considering where we are," Piper said determined to pull herself together.

"Cowboys have lumps of lead for brains, but mercy." The vibrant redhead with the laughing eyes did a little dance move that verged on scandalous. "They make up for it in other areas."

Piper stared at her. It was just so bizarre, her appearing like an angel. She'd always loved how tight-knit the rodeo community was. But this woman seemed instantly like she could be a friend, like Piper could count on her to understand.

"I'm afraid so."

Boone's "other areas" of expertise had definitely made her lose all sense of her goals. The woman looked at her phone. Then she sent a quick text.

"OK, I have twenty minutes. Let's have a drink at the Graff—we'll have more P and Q and Shane."

Piper stared—not really sure what P or Q was, and she'd never met a Shane, except one of the cowboys was named Shane Marvell—a marvelous name, Piper punned but didn't want to confide in one of Boone's friends.

"P and Q?" she asked faintly.

"Privacy and quiet. I'm Tucker Wilder, and we can compare notes because, girl, I have done my share of heartbreaks on cowboys and they've done a number on me, but I can testify." She held up her hand like she was taking an oath. "Some cowboys are worth the grief and others just aren't."

"Are you related to Kane Wilder?" Piper asked.

"God, help us all that I am. He's my brother-in-law." Tucker shook her head. "I have no idea why Sky, his wife, doesn't brain him with a frying pan most days for trying to tell us all what we should do and constantly flaunting his perfection and discipline in our faces. He caused his share of heartbreak in the day, but duller than a dead-headed daisy now. I got the best Wilder brother. He makes whiskey and thinks I walk on water, which I do just to keep him in line."

Piper blinked at her, and Tucker smiled. "No worries. I'm an acquired taste. Now tell me about your cowboy. How did he F-bomb up this time?"

Piper sighed. "It's not Boone's fault exactly," Piper said without thinking but something about the young woman who just snap, crackled and oozed confidence had Piper confessing.

"Boone Telford?"

Of course she knew him. For all Piper knew this beautiful woman was an ex-cheerleader or rodeo queen girlfriend or his junior year prom date or…

Tucker texted again. "Okay, I've told Shane to expect us and she's concocting her magic. My sister Tanner is a stock contractor with the rodeo, and she's going to cover for me for a few and you are going to dish."

"I really don't think…" Piper broke off when Tucker tucked her wiry arm through hers and began to speed-walk across the bridge toward Crawford Park and Main Street.

"Don't think, just spew dirt because if Boone Telford has made a girl cry, Mercury must be seriously in retrograde or Orion's taking off his belt or Uranus and Mars are spatting… Maybe we should all buy lottery tickets."

"I'm not…" Piper continued to walk with Tucker because she was curious and no longer felt like sobbing her heart out onto the pavement, but she had no intention of airing her problems to a stranger. "It's not fair to Boone if I…"

"All's fair in love and war or so I've heard," Tucker said. "And Boone is golden. He's actually called that. The golden one because he's so sweet and perfect. He's the sun, and I was the black cloud of the town growing up."

"Oh, you grew up in Marietta too?" This was going to be bad, but Tucker was a force of nature, and Piper just felt sadly in need of a friend to provide some female perspective.

"Born and bred and couldn't wait to leave—only now I'm back to stay," Tucker said as they mounted the graceful, half-circle staircase leading up to the Graff Hotel that Piper had noticed yesterday. "Nothing like a lot of distance to make your heart grow fonder."

Distance had never made anyone grow fonder of her, Piper thought, feeling despair creep back through the protective walls she was trying to build.

They entered the hotel, but Piper didn't notice the décor. She needed something, anything to distract herself.

"Were you and Boone a…you know?"

Tucker laughed. "That would have been something. The former town bad girl and the golden one, but no. I was out of here before he hit high school. My family and I are working with his family's ranch. Expanding operations."

The reality of the breakup was beginning to hit, and Piper was starting to think a drink, even though it was barely noon, might be a good idea. She didn't think she had any clients booked until later, but screw it if she did. She'd never been irresponsible in her life. Maybe today was the day.

"It's ironic, that I was once such a heartbreaker because now I am a heart-healer. It's my gift to the world."

Piper found herself smiling. Tucker was pretty outrageous, but Piper thought if she were alone with everything howling around inside of her, she'd never stop crying. And she was not a crier. She was a pick-myself-up-and-get-on-with-it woman.

She followed Tucker across the airy lobby to a pub-style bar tucked toward the back. A tall, gorgeous blonde woman was shaking two silver shakers. She looked confident and sexy behind the beautiful, long, dark wood bar.

"Have a seat." She smiled at them both. Her expression was warm and her light blue eyes seemed to glow. "New recipe I'm trying out at Tucker's request. Guaranteed to soothe even the achiest heartbreak."

The bartender, who must be Shane, flipped two cocktail napkins toward them and then poured out a golden concoction into their glasses. She then added a squirt of something red, and a slice of candied ginger and a fresh cherry.

"I don't know about that," Piper said. "You're making me feel melodramatic." She took a deep breath and looked around the small bar. She caught a glimpse of a gift store that looked a little like an art gallery beyond the bar and then she looked back at the two smiling women. Clearly they were friends. Clearly they belonged. She just had to keep looking. Have faith.

She took up the cocktail. "To the journey," she said, really wishing she meant it.

BOONE STOOD OUTSIDE the chute waiting for his turn. Usually he loved this feeling—the adrenaline coursing through his body. The focus. The way his vision tunneled and calm descended almost like he was underwater. And he'd picture his ride. Each step planned out.

Now all he saw was Piper. Green eyes brilliant, slashing away her tears.

He'd hurt her.

Focus.

Unacceptable.

He sucked in a breath. Three cowboys ahead.

Focus on the goddamn ride. Slip in the zone.

Piper.

Usually it was effortless, this part. Every cowboy had their ritual. Boone was a million miles away from his, and that could spell disaster. And he didn't give a shit. But he had to because he had to survive this, he had to kill it, so he could find Piper, and find the words that would make his actions, and all these dumbass feelings he'd been swatting away make sense.

His dad was there. Silent. Worried. He knew he was

fucking up. Hell, the whole town would know it in another minute.

No.

Focus.

He could do this. He'd done it again and again. Total concentration, head nod, scream out of the chute, leap grab, twist, roll. A few seconds where nothing—doubt, self-recrimination, goals—would interfere.

His dad's presence barely registered, but he squeezed Boone's shoulder.

"Want me to talk to them about moving you later?" his dad asked.

Boone shook his head. "I'm good," he lied.

"You could scratch."

"No." Boone drew himself up. "Not scratching. Never scratching."

He was going to drop that steer then man the fuck up and find Piper. He needed to know she was okay. She deserved so much better than what he'd given her.

"Boone, I can see it in your eyes, your body, you're not ready. I think…"

"Dad." Boone stared his father straight in the eye. His dad had been the most important person in his life. His inspiration. His role model. But he couldn't fix this. And even if he could, Boone wouldn't let him. Piper was his. She would always be his even if she'd never talk to him again.

And he always took care of his own.

That realization hit him like a fist.

Piper was his the way his family was his.

And he'd been too much of a coward to admit it to himself, but even worse, he hadn't told her. Ever.

And he couldn't. Not now. He didn't deserve her. Not yet. He might never. But he could do his damn best to become a man who would deserve Piper. And that had to start here. Now.

"You're on deck," one of the chute hands shouted down at him.

"Boone," his father said tersely.

Boone gripped his dad's shoulder like his dad had done to him so many times. His dad was nearly fifty-three, yet he still had a wiry strength due to his daily work on the ranch that would be admirable in men half his age. It was a hard life, but a good one.

"I've got this."

He didn't back down from a challenge. Not ever. And he wasn't going to start today. And he wasn't going to run from his problems with Piper anymore.

Boone pulled off his gloves and put them back on again. Stamped his right foot twice—then twice left. Jammed his hat down lower on his head. Then rolled his head right then left. Feeling the calm settle over him. The determination. He led Sundance to the chute. Clamored up and dropped down.

He blocked out the roar of the crowd. Nothing mattered but twisting that steer to the ground and getting the hell out of the arena.

Usually Will Reeves rode alongside to hem in the steer, but today his father had asked if he could partner up with Boone this round, and since his father was on the rodeo committee and he and Boone's mother and a handful of other locals had spear-headed the rebuilding campaign, it wasn't like anyone was going to say no.

The crowd was loud. Boone barely noticed. He nodded. The bolt of the chute slid free and simultaneously, he and Sundance, a small steer and his father on a horse burst out of the chutes. Boone immediately jumped, dropped, grabbed the steer's horns and twisted as he rolled: 3.2. Incredible time. Even Boone snapped out of his misery for a moment to stare in awe at the number. He'd have an impossible time matching it, much less beating it if he competed another five years.

His dad was smiling. One fist pump in the air. Wild acclaim from his understated dad. Feeling like a robot Boone tipped his hat to the hometown audience. He spotted his mom, sister, sister-in-law and brother in the crowd holding signs. He briefly waved. Smiled on autopilot and then jumped the fence.

Time to finally stop living his life moment by moment.

Time to become a man with a plan.

Chapter Ten

BOONE MUST BE flying high, Piper thought Saturday night while she anxiously scanned the crowd starting to line up for the first steaks coming off the barbeque pits. He was in first place by a lot going into the steer wrestling and also was tied for second going into bareback bronc and bull riding short round tomorrow.

Initially she had wanted to finalize their breakup in the trailer, but somehow having a crowd made her feel less emotionally exposed. And raw. The day had passed in a blur, and she still hadn't completely sorted through her feelings. First the early drink with Tucker, who'd been so funny, friendly and wise even when she made outrageous statements. Piper rarely drank alcohol, especially during the day on an empty stomach. Luckily Shane had gone super light on the alcohol, heavier on the kindness and friendship.

Neither of the women had pushed for details of the 'cowboy problem,' as Tucker had called it, which had surprised and pleased Piper. But she had felt comforted. And knew that no matter how much it hurt now, no matter how long, she would survive. Not close down and turn away from love like her mother had. And her father.

Tucker had sat at the Graff's beautiful dark wood bar and diagnosed the problem with minimal information as "Boone is head over heels but without a clue." Tucker had popped open the pistachio nut shells from a bowl on the bar with her thumb and forefinger and tossed the nuts up into the air, and they'd fallen into her mouth with envying accuracy. Piper hadn't been able to do much but nurse her drink and try to keep her mind on the conversation between the two women who were clearly good friends, even though Shane had said she was leaving town a week or so after the rodeo.

"Typical cowboy," Tucker said with authority. "Add in the fact that he just turned twenty-five. His frontal lobe is barely coalesced."

That had amused Shane to the point of snorting.

"That's sexist," Piper had roused herself to protest. Besides, why had they assumed everything was Boone's fault? It wasn't. Piper had participated in her own crash and burn. She'd jumped all in. Hadn't asked enough questions.

Because, let's face it, she'd told herself sternly, she'd been afraid of his answers.

"Boohoo. Let's start a new hashtag #DumbInLoveCowboy."

"Probably a million tweets for that one, judging from what I hear in my bar, and I don't even work the cowboy bar, Grey's," Shane had said before waving them off with a smile and exchanging numbers.

Tucker had to return to the rodeo to help her sister and their stock hands. Piper hadn't quite felt ready for that, but she had, after some encouragement, agreed to sit with Tucker's family during the steak dinner.

"Unless you get a better offer." Tucker had winked.

"Not holding my breath," Piper had breathed, deciding to walk Main Street, weigh her options, and ignore the texts she could feel buzzing in her pocket.

She had checked the rodeo stats to make sure Boone hadn't been injured.

No. He was thriving. Scoring crazy high. Clearly not impacted by their breakup. He was probably relieved.

"I'm going to be fine," Piper had said as she'd walked unerringly toward the Copper Mountain Chocolate shop again where she would not, absolutely would not buy another box of cowboy boot chocolates. Until she did, so distracted by her own personal hurt, she'd practically snatched the last small box out of the hands of an adorable little boy. Mortified, Piper had tried to hand the box back, but the mother had politely refused. Piper asked if she could share the chocolate with them—something the little boy, Ricky, had loved. They'd walked a few blocks together. The mom, Kelly, had been nice, but thoughts of Boone kept dragging Piper out of the conversation.

Piper forced herself back into the present. She'd managed

to avoid Boone today—not easy as she hadn't realized how dogged he could be when thwarted—but she'd felt the need to armor herself. Make a plan. So she'd agreed to meet him at the steak dinner, but still had no idea of what she would say.

God, this was so hard.

Excruciatingly painful.

And she felt like the steak dinner, the town, the people jostling together greeting each other mocked the dreams she'd clung to all her life. Marietta was everything she'd ever hoped for in a hometown. Boone was everything she'd wanted in a man. And she stood here alone, empty-handed. Again.

Piper balled her fists.

She was not giving up. Who knew? If she decided to stay in Marietta, start her own business, put down roots, she might be here next year greeting friends—for once part of the small-town charm, absorbing the sweetness and magic. The lights strung through the trees in the park gave off a golden glow that seemed like it could only be created on a movie set. Around her conversations flowed. The opening band was tuning up; the smell of barbeque permeated the air all around them. And then she saw him.

Boone.

Her heart hitched and sped up just like it did the first time.

He looked invincible. So strong and appealing and handsome. He moved through the crowd with a fluidity she'd always admired. And he was coming toward her. Piper could barely breathe. She had to stay strong. Not give in. Although maybe there was nothing to give in to. Oh, she knew he'd never throw her out. He'd help her find a place to stay or let her sleep in the trailer while he went to his family's ranch.

Her heart clenched.

This was it.

Only it wasn't. Boone was stopped. Again. And again. By a few families with older teens, by couples, by older men. And each time he listened, his face open, friendly, but she could see the tension in his shoulders, in the tightness of his back.

He was coming to find her.

But he was too polite to brush off the people who knew him, who wanted to congratulate him, who wanted to catch up because he hadn't been home in four months because he'd been traveling with her—showing her the American west instead of his real life.

Suddenly it was too much.

She didn't want to do this now.

She didn't think she'd ever be up to it.

Who knew love could hurt like this?

She was looking at the truth. Boone belonged. She'd seen it this afternoon when she'd caught a glimpse of Boone at the cowboy's autograph booth. Fans and friends were happy to see him, and Boone seemed to know so many of them, seemed to enjoy spending an hour greeting people and signing programs and T-shirts and hats. Often he scooped up the smaller kids or bent to their level and greeted them personally. Marietta was his home even if he had been temporarily running away from it. He belonged to his marrow.

She could belong too—in her own way, not his—make her own world day by day. And today was her day one.

Piper turned away, texting Tucker to see if she'd arrived and if the invitation to sit with them was still open. Tucker's text, and a picture of where she was, came through immediately. Piper gulped in a breath, cast one last, no doubt longing look at Boone and then turned away, walking quickly to join Tucker, her husband and the rest of her family and friends in line. They'd already reserved a table and there was plenty of room.

One friend. That was all she needed to start. But she had something more.

As she walked, she scrolled down to Amanda's number. She paused. Was she really ready for this? Did she have a choice?

Tears blinding her, she looked up from her phone as if seeking inspiration. She hadn't realized she was so near the makeshift stage and dance floor until she heard a singer she'd heard performing yesterday tune up his guitar and greet the crowd. He was handsome and confident although he made self-deprecating remarks about how he knew he wasn't the opening act, but he was "going to try to entertain y'all anyway. Keep this stage up here warm and welcoming," he said into the mic.

The crowd, most of them milling around and starting to make their way toward the lines for food, certainly seemed welcoming. People called out his name. Cheered. Made song suggestions.

The music started. He was good. Piper didn't recognize the song, but she hadn't listened to much country before Boone. She wondered if the musician wrote it himself. A couple went up to the stage. The woman was beautiful—loads of dark, wavy hair and a beautiful red dress that hugged her figure. The cowboy, Flynn, she now realized, certainly seemed enamored. The way he held the woman and looked down at her, his face lit with intent and caring.

Piper swallowed hard. She thought she had that with Boone.

She'd been wrong.

And she wasn't going to make the same mistake over and over. She'd promised herself growing up that she'd find a place that felt like home. Have a family she loved and who loved her back. She'd vowed it when she went to college. Had realized she'd never have it if she stayed with her traveling dance company. And Boone had veered her off course again.

Piper looked back at Amanda's number and quickly typed out a simple sentence. She stared at it. So little to mean so much.

Piper hit send.

DAMN, WHERE WAS Piper? She'd finally answered one of his ten thousand texts and said she'd meet him at the steak dinner. He'd busted ass after his bull ride. Of course he'd drawn late in the competition. Good for morale to watch cowboy after cowboy get tossed into the dirt, or bad depending on the cowboy's confidence level.

But Boone had felt fierce. Determined to ride to the bell. See Piper.

He also had admitted to himself when he'd been so restless backstage that he'd been hoping like hell Piper would show, even though he knew he had no right.

Still.

But he'd showered in record time, changed into a shirt Piper had chosen for him in Telluride, Colorado, checked on Sundance and hurried to the steak dinner.

She must be here. He tried to quell the unaccustomed anxiety. He'd checked her tent and their trailer. That pretty blue halter-style sundress she'd bought one afternoon when they were sight-seeing and kayaking in Cherry Lake a couple of weeks ago was gone from the closet.

He admitted to himself he'd been relieved that was all that was missing.

Boone squared his shoulders and palmed the two plates

of food. She wasn't in line. But he didn't imagine she'd be sitting down. Piper didn't like to eat alone. She'd confessed one night that she didn't even like to sit in a coffee shop by herself.

Boone had thought it so sweet. And sad. And then he'd stupidly pulled her close and said, "Now you don't have to. You have me."

Dumb ass.

He thought he'd been preparing to cut her loose.

Instead he'd been pulling her close.

While pushing her away, making her do his dirty work.

He heard his name called yet again, but he kept walking determinedly toward an unfixed destination in the crowd. At this rate, dinner and dancing would be over before he found her because so many people wanted to stop and talk.

"Hey, Boone," he heard his sister-in-law, Miranda, call his name.

"Hi," he said automatically not really looking at her, still scanning for Piper.

"Over here. We didn't save you a seat because we thought you'd be with your parents, but you can have mine so you can eat your meal. That's a lot of food. How are you going to eat all that?"

"It's not all for me." He met Miranda's amused pixie face tolerantly. "Obviously."

"Well, you and your invisible friend can have my seat. I'm going for another margarita or two so I can enjoy the show."

"What show?" He didn't really think of eating dinner and country dancing as a show, but there was usually a bit of drama at the rodeo, especially at the steak dinner.

She moved toward the alcohol tent, and he found himself staring at Piper. She was sitting at the table with the Wilders, Shane Knight—the bartender at the Graff—and a few other ranch friends. He jerked in surprise and only years of balancing on the back on an animal that was trying to hurl him off kept the plates steady in his hands. He suddenly felt totally nervous, like he had the first time he'd met her.

Piper regarded him coolly, almost as if he were a stranger, and then she picked up her half corn on the cob and took a bite.

A little butter smeared on her lips.

Jesus, she looked beautiful.

And unapproachable. She might as well be sitting on top of Copper Mountain.

He just stood there probably looking stupid. With two plates of food.

Everyone stopped eating and talking and looked up at him. He nodded stiffly to Kane and his wife, Sky. Then Kane's brothers, Luke and Laird, and their wives Tanner and Tucker, who'd recently started working with his father's ranch. Colt Wilder and his wife Talon, who had one more year of vet school left, sat on the other side of Piper, leaving a place next to her if he squeezed in on the end across from

Shane, who looked about as impressed with him as he felt—lower than low.

"Piper." He stood awkward, not sure of his welcome, but determined not to leave.

She hesitated. And then looked up. He saw a quick flash of anguish before she shut it down.

"Congratulations," she said, her voice so low he had to strain to hear her. "Great scores. Short round in each event."

He didn't want to talk about the rodeo.

But it was a start.

"Did you watch?" he couldn't help asking even though he knew he shouldn't hope.

Piper shook her head quickly. "Online leader board," she said looking at anyone but him.

"Hey, cowboy," Tucker called out, tossing her long auburn mane of hair over her shoulder like a taunt. "Pull up a saddle. Meet my new friend Piper, out of the closet and a shitload of fun."

Tucker toasted him with a glass of whiskey from a bottle that had the Wilder Whiskey label her husband had started as a lark one winter and was now building fast. Boone was pretty sure bringing a bottle of whiskey to a public park was not legal, but Tucker had never been one for following rules.

Boone folded himself into a chair, willing Piper to look at him. He tried to puzzle out how she knew the Wilders, Shane and Miranda.

And no one, including his sister-in-law, usually the sunniest of people, seemed particularly happy to see him.

"Oh, Boone, hello. I didn't know you knew Piper." Laird joined in his wife's fun proving that they were well matched.

Boone tried to catch Piper's eye, but she was slathering butter on a corn bread muffin. He'd never even seen her eat bread or butter so this was bad. Real bad. And he had to make sure she was okay, settled somewhere she wanted to be before he got too involved in the ranch or headed out to Great Falls to compete next weekend.

"How was your day?" The minute he uttered the trite, everyday question, he winced.

Piper shot him a look.

Boone thought and re-thought what he should say. And his food grew cold. The steak, potato, corn and mixture of several salads he'd piled on looked unappealing, and his stomach swirled sickly, but he knew he needed fuel for tomorrow.

And tonight was going to be long. Lonely.

But then a shaft of hope shot through his dread when Piper's knee brushed against his. She jumped in her seat, but didn't move her leg. Boone tried not to read anything into it.

The conversations turned to the rodeo, bulls, Tucker wanting to start breeding and training bucking broncos.

"Because then you could give me a heart attack every few minutes instead of a few a day," Laird muttered.

Tucker laughed. "It's another gift." She kissed her husband's cheek. "Or maybe now it's a skill. Probably the one

I'm best at."

"I don't know." Her twin smiled. "You're getting pretty dang comfortable with the bull-breeding operation."

"Piper." Tucker sat up straight, her eyes sparkled, and her mouth curved in a you're-so-fucked curve that Boone was really hoping was directed at her sister, not at him. Luke and Laird groaned, but Tucker continued enthusiastically. "You haven't lived until you've jacked off a bull. I showed Shane how. She was all in. Started thinking of giving up bartending. Life-changing experience. Plus, you could help create the monsters that will toss stupid-ass, arrogant cowboys on their dumb asses in front of a crowd. Sell tickets."

Boone tossed his napkin on his plate.

"Okay, Tucker," he heard her twin Tanner say quietly. Tanner had always been the nicer one. "You made your point."

Tucker's eyes squinted in challenge. Boone faced her. He'd been a jackass. He could handle anything Tucker could dish out, but he didn't want Piper hurt. Or embarrassed.

"You want to talk directly to me?" he asked Tucker quietly.

"It's okay, Tucker, really," Piper said softly, the husk in her voice pronounced.

Boone jerked restlessly. Piper was a million miles from okay, and he was a million further.

Shane poured herself a finger of whiskey. Then she poured another finger in a shot glass and scooted it down to

Boone. He stared at it. What? They wanted him to get drunk and thrown tomorrow because he'd been an idiot about Piper, wanting to keep her close even as he knew he had to cut her loose? Wanting to keep her for himself even though he knew she was too good for him? Get in line. He was beating himself up enough.

"I don't…"

"You're gonna want it tonight," Shane said and hoisted up her shot and threw it down her throat.

"I need to learn how to do that." Piper leaned on her elbow, food forgotten as she watched Shane toss back the shot. Boone could swear he saw admiration cross her beautiful features.

What. The. Hell?

He'd barely seen Piper drink, much less shoot whiskey.

"I can teach you," Tucker called out. "Any night of the week."

"Tucker's got the advanced degree," Talon said, looking around her husband, Colt, to grin at Piper. She ran her hand through her long, spiral blonde curls. "I still choke doing it. Maybe we could practice together."

Like Piper was going to have time for that, Boone thought moodily. He hoped she wasn't too shocked by the conversation, and he opened his mouth to tell her they were teasing—at least he hoped they were—but Piper was listening. Her eyes sparkled and looked a little dreamy. She swirled the large ice cubes in her drink, and Boone realized with a start that it was a margarita from Rosita's. And there was an empty glass beside her. And a nearly full plate of food.

Shit. When he fucked up, he did it but good. Piper was a light-weight.

Miranda returned holding two margaritas. "Here you go, Piper."

"I'll find you a chair." Colt rose up quickly, a mountain of a man full of purpose.

"No need," Boone said pushing back from his full two plates of food more aggressively than he meant to. The chair tipped backward, and he didn't even pick it up. Instead he picked up the shot glass, mock toasted Shane, who stared at him stonily. Subtly flipped off Tucker while holding the glass.

"So hurt." She laughed at him.

Boone ignored her and tossed back the whiskey.

Fuck, Laird knew what he was doing. Boone craved another shot. He needed it. But he was manning up now. This was between him and Piper. Not his family. Not his so-called friends and definitely not his family's business partners.

"Anyone teaching Piper to drink whiskey's it's me," he said. "Let's dance."

HE DIDN'T GIVE her much choice. And Piper knew she

should say no. Or at least put up some sort of resistance, but Boone laced his fingers with hers and walked her through several long rows of tables as he made his way toward the band and the dance floor, and really, Piper just wanted to curl in to his body and cling. It felt so good to be connected after feeling adrift all day.

Her body felt warm and liquid as she admired the familiar line of his back—the silky black shirt with the white piping across his broad shoulders. He wore jet-black Wranglers and shined cowboy boots.

Don't look at him, she ordered herself.

It was just the tequila talking.

She was over Boone Telford. So over.

Except when they reached the dance floor, the main band was already moving into their second song, and Boone swung around, his body already set, and Piper rested her hand on his hip, and let him take her other hand.

Wrong. Wrong. Wrong.

Except it felt so right when he began to move, and she followed his moves as if connected by invisible threads. He'd left the two top buttons of his shirt open creating a deep V that revealed his throat and his chest, and her heart squeezed.

"You look beautiful, Piper," he said, his voice low and serious. His gaze grave.

"Don't say that," she whispered back.

"It's true. Most beautiful girl here."

"You can't talk like that to me anymore."

"Can't help it."

He was so good at this, Piper despaired, making her feel special, when clearly she wasn't. He'd made his choice, and it definitely wasn't her.

And still, he didn't miss a beat, effortlessly steering her around the floor, dodging the couples without looking.

She should run. But another part of her wanted to remember this—how Boone looked when he gazed at her. How his body felt brushing against hers as he'd spin her or turn her to promenade. Memories were all she'd have, and she needed to store each one up.

"I know we need to talk," Boone said.

She stared down at the tips of the turquoise boots he'd bought her in Missoula. She didn't know if she'd wear them again. Too many memories. She'd store them in the box, maybe high on a shelf—perhaps even in the studio over a garage apartment Shane, who was leaving Marietta in a couple of weeks, had offered her. Perhaps she'd take them out in a year or two when it didn't hurt so much. Wear them to another rodeo steak dinner when she could actually appreciate the beauty of the night, the food, the conversation without everything aching so much inside she could barely stand up straight, much less dance.

"Piper I'm sorry." He bent down, trying to look into her eyes, but she kept her gaze glued to her boots.

Now that he was here, his attention on her, she wanted to forget about what he'd done, pretend it didn't matter, just dance with him, let him make love to her one last time. She hated how much she wanted him to hold her. Her father had said love made you weak. Piper felt so weak, but she didn't want the colonel to be right.

She hated how easily she'd fallen in love.

And how easy it had been for him to keep her separate from his real life.

She'd been more temporary than she'd realized.

And now she was a burden because Boone was a nice man who wouldn't just walk off into the sunset with a head bob of 'thanks, see ya around.' He'd want to help her get to where she wanted to go.

Only she didn't want to go anywhere.

And she didn't want to make her new life without him.

The song ended and the next flowed into a slow, haunting melody. Boone gathered her close, and Piper, weak, let herself melt into him. Her fingers touched the onyx snaps on his shirt.

She felt like she was about to crack open and only him holding her tightly would keep her in one piece.

Was it wrong to wish?

Was it wrong to hope?

Piper closed her eyes and willed the moment to last, but she knew what she had to do. She'd wanted Boone to be honest with her, and yet she needed to be honest with herself.

It was all so clear now. The inequity. Her feelings compared to his.

"You don't need to apologize," Piper said, forcing herself to look him in his beautiful blue eyes. "I'm the one who broke the rule."

"The rule?"

"You were honest from the beginning. You offered a summer of fun, but for me, it became more than fun a long time ago."

She reached up and traced his brow and across his high cheekbone that always made her tummy flip. Then she smoothed her thumb over his lip. Maybe the last time she'd ever get to touch him.

"I should be the one apologizing. I changed."

"Piper." He caught her hands in his and held them to his chest. He'd done that so many times—holding her hands to his heart. How she wished she could hold his heart. Be his.

"I'm going to miss you, Boone." Piper sucked up her courage and her pride. She wasn't her father's daughter for nothing. She'd been rejected before for reasons both in and out of her control. And it would happen again. She'd survive. That was also what she did. Time and time again.

"It's okay. I know you don't…feel the same, but I…" She wanted to tell him. Love was a beautiful feeling even when it hurt. And Boone deserved love.

The music kept playing soft and sweet. Couples brushed against them as they swayed past. The fairy lights strung up in the trees overhead coupled with the distant conversation made everything seem a little dreamy.

"I love you. I wanted you to know. But…" How did she get the words out when she felt like she was dying inside? "We need to be over."

He still held her hands. She could feel his heart pound like a wild thing.

"Piper, I never…"

She pressed two fingers against his lips, not wanting to hear his next words, not wanting her fears confirmed. She loved him. He didn't love her. Story of her life.

But she was going to change her story.

"I love you, Boone. I think I will always love you, but I can't be with you anymore."

The ballad ended, and the space between the last note and the first of the next song seemed to stretch forever. Boone looked as tortured as she felt. He blurred before her like a watercolor in the rain.

It was over. It hit her like a dump truck. Completely over and the last hope flickered out that he'd protest. Tell her that he loved her too. That he couldn't imagine his life without her.

Piper pressed her lips together and kept her eyes from blinking because then the tears would fall.

"Thank you, Boone, for an amazing summer and showing me Montana and so much more."

She spun around and walked away fast. She didn't even know where she was going. Everything looked underwater.

She couldn't go back to the tables. She couldn't face anyone until she'd had a pathetic sob fest and then pulled herself together. Piper hopped over a grouping of hay bales and skirted around some trees before she heard the babble of the Marietta River.

Usually water soothed her, but Piper had a feeling it would be a long time before she could feel soothed. But in a way she was proud. She'd deeply loved a man. And she'd had the strength to let him go so that she could eventually find her own home and her own happiness even if it was alone. And she'd left Boone's heart whole. He would be free to find what he was so desperately looking for. He'd be free to find the woman of his dreams.

She was full-on hiccupping ugly sobs by the time she made it to the bridge. And she was running even though Boone wasn't chasing her. Oh. God. What was he thinking? Feeling? He must be so relieved to get rid of her. He'd tried to show her and tell her in so many ways this weekend.

Piper bit back a scream of anger at herself. She was having a breakdown over a man. Something she never thought she'd do. She'd told Boone she loved him, and he'd just looked stricken. Piper stumbled toward the grandstand thinking she could hide under it. But she stopped uncertainly. She heard people, whispers, breathing, a soft moan.

That's all she needed, to witness someone else's personal bliss. Piper scurried away. She'd go to the trailer. Pack. But the burst of will that had helped her to rip open her heart on the dance floor for Boone's dismayed and embarrassed perusal, before cutting him free, had deserted her. She could barely lift her key to unlock the door. She struggled with the lock and then fell inside. She slammed the door, locked it and pressed back against it.

"Think. Think." She dashed her hands over her eyes.

She hated crying. It was weak and unproductive. Her father's words. Cold. But practical. Besides she didn't cry pretty and she was always blotchy and swollen the next day so she had to stop now. Piper gulped in a few breaths while her eyes seemed to ping-pong around the small space that had been home for four months.

Squaring her shoulders, she pulled her duffel bag out from the bottom of the small closet. And her backpack. She traveled light. Often. This part, the physical part—picking up and leaving—she was so damn good at it.

Chapter Eleven

BOONE WATCHED PIPER'S back as she hurried through the crowd. Usually she was so graceful when she moved, and he'd find himself staring at her like she'd cast a spell on him. But now her movements were slightly jerky, and her shoulders hunched. She was practically running, and her red-blonde hair bounced down her bare back as if urging her to move faster.

She loved him.

She'd told him that she loved him, and he'd just stood there. He couldn't love Piper. He couldn't. What did he have to offer her? Fun times and great sex.

Piper deserved the world. The home and family and sense of belonging she'd always missed. He needed to let her go, but as he watched her hurry through the crowd and then clamor over the hay bales and disappear toward the small copse of trees by the Marietta River, all he could think of was how small and vulnerable and alone she looked.

And he'd done that to her.

"Hey, Telford, stop pretending to be a damn cowboy

sculpture and get off the dance floor." Cody deliberately shoulder-checked him as he spun that pretty girl Boone had seen him with a few times this weekend: Kelly. She must be the one Cody had done right with his prize money. He'd seen her holding the hand of a cute kid. She was already looking at Cody with stars in her eyes.

"You gotta ask a girl to dance. You can't just stand here looking stupid and hope some gorgeous girl takes pity on your sorry ass."

"I've been dumped," Boone tested the words.

"Wait." Cody stopped dancing and his arm snaked around his partner and he tucked her close to his side. "By Piper?"

He nodded. He took off his hat and ran his hand through his hair and then stared at his fingers. They were shaking. Shaking. "She told me she loved me," he told Cody feeling hollow inside.

He dropped his hat but made no move to pick it up. Couples moved around them, but Boone felt like he was seeing it all from far away. Even the music, voices and laughter seemed muffled.

Kelly bent down and retrieved his hat. She held it out to him, but he hardly noticed.

Cody shifted his weight. Pulled off his own cowboy hat, spun it around his hand once. Opened his mouth to speak. Spun it again and then jammed his Stetson back on his head.

"That's good right?" He sounded as lost as Boone felt. "I

mean she's been traveling with you for, what, like four or five months now? She adores you. Everyone could tell. Hell, her face lights up every time you saunter up like you own the whole place and everyone's just waiting for you to arrive."

"Well, she was running away tonight." Boone could hardly speak around the lump in his throat. He tried to swallow. "Why the hell would she love me?"

"You going after her?"

"Pretty sure that's the last thing she wants, but yeah I need to."

"Need or want?"

"What's the difference?"

"You love her? Tell her. If not…" Cody shrugged.

"It's not that easy," Boone said still staring off in the direction where Piper had fled as if chased by demons. "It's complicated."

And he didn't do complicated.

Ever.

But he couldn't let Piper go. Not like that. Not thinking he didn't give a damn. Boone jammed his Stetson on his head.

"Later, man," he said already striding away.

It took him twenty agonizing minutes to find her. Even when he went to her massage tent, he didn't spot her right away. It was more like he felt her there. And he'd stood quietly, absorbing the smell of the grass, the lingering scent of the oil she used, and the hint of the elusive scent of Piper.

"Piper," he said softly, looking around. It was dark. And quiet. But he felt her. "Piper. Baby?"

"Please go, Boone," she whispered.

She was crying. He heard a gulp and a muffled sniff and the rustle of material. Damn. He really was a dick. To Piper. Who'd only given him total acceptance and a happiness he hadn't known had existed outside the thrill of pitting his strength and skills against a beast at the rodeo.

His eyes adjusted to the darkness in the tent. Piper wasn't on the massage table, she was huddled under it, and Boone felt like all the blood in his body just whooshed out of him leaving him cold and numb and aching.

"Piper, baby." He knew she wouldn't come out.

So he went to her. Not easy bending six-foot plus of his body under the low bed, but he did it and scooted over to sit cautiously beside her. Piper held herself rigidly and leaned away from him. And after a few seconds, Boone couldn't take the distance. He slipped his arm around her.

"Piper," he breathed.

She folded herself in to him, and Boone stretched out his legs and pulled her close. It was damned cramped underneath the table, but nothing had felt as right as Piper in his arms. His hands smoothed over her body and he kissed her tangled hair that fell all around them. He'd always loved how the strands would catch in the scruff that he had by the end of the night—connecting them.

He inhaled her delicate scent—lightly floral—

honeysuckle—and lemon. She reminded him of sunshine, but her arms were chilled. He rubbed his hand back and forth over her bare arms and wished he'd brought his jacket to the dinner.

"Sorry," Piper said for like the fifth time. "I'm sorry. I promised myself I wouldn't cry. I don't want you to feel bad."

Bad was an understatement. He felt like fucking hell.

"Piper, baby, this kills me. I never meant to hurt you."

"I know."

He could feel her trembling against him, trying to choke back her sobs. He stroked his hand over her back and held her close, wanting to warm her, soothe her. And hell if he knew how he was going to let her go.

He closed his eyes, so exhausted he wasn't even sure if he could find the energy to stand up and get them both home. That was it, wasn't it? Piper had become his home—not Marietta, not the ranch, not the trailer, not even his family. None of it would be home without Piper.

"Let me just hold you," he whispered.

For a little while until you feel better.

He wanted to fix this. He always fixed things—broken farm equipment, engines, tractors, motors of all sorts. Anything mechanical, he was the man, but with broken hearts, broken dreams, he was helpless. Useless.

"It will be that much harder when you let go." Her voice was as broken as he felt.

She was right. Of course she was. Far off he could hear the strains of the band, and he thought the melodic rumble of the crowd, and closer the hum of the last of the season's crickets and Piper's hiccupping sobs.

"We were good together, baby."

"I need more than good, Boone. I need more than today and maybe tomorrow."

He nodded.

"I have goals for myself, and I was hoping that my goals aligned with yours, and seeing this town, knowing that you grew up here and that you have a family and a ranch here just made me see that even though you have roots, you don't want to put any down with me."

Her voice ached. He ached.

"Oh, Piper. It's not like that at all," he said, letting his mouth rest against his silky hair. "You're perfect. I've been the luckiest idiot ever that you even looked my way. It's just that my life has been handed to me. Everything prescribed. So much history. So much legacy. My parents are so in love. They are the best. My dad is my hero. He's accomplished so much, and I'm just his son."

Piper finally looked at him. Her mouth was a whisper away from his.

"I don't understand. Why doesn't that make you happy?"

He huffed out a hollow laugh. "That's the worst part of it, baby. I just can't explain it, but everything that's considered mine, my legacy, my future, was created by my parents. I need to know who I am separate from them. And if I come home and work the ranch again, I want to bring something with me. Something that's just me."

"Like what?"

He let her question settle into him. That was it, wasn't it? The crux. The million-dollar question.

"Land? Prize money? Buckles? How many?" Piper asked.

"I don't know."

"Do you even want to work the ranch? You said you didn't want to go to college. Would you rather go into stock contracting? Announcing? Promotion?"

"Piper, I don't know."

"How can you achieve something if you don't know what it is?"

Her words hit with the power of a hoof to his sternum.

"See that's just it, Boone. I don't care about any of that, and I think your parents are the same." Piper scooted onto her knees and held his face between her two chilled hands. "I love you as you are. I don't need you to be anything else, accomplish anything else. I love the man before me. I love you when you win and when you lose. I love you when you're happy and fun and when you're quiet and withdrawn. But if you are going to hold yourself to a standard of accomplishment, you need to know what it is. You can't achieve something you can't articulate. How can you know when you've climbed your peak, if you can't see it?"

She leaned forward and kissed his mouth, sweetly.

"I want you to achieve your dreams, Boone. I want you to feel like you've made your mark, and I'd love it to be with me, but until you know what you want, you can't be the man you want to be."

"I know."

"But if you remember nothing else about me, know that I love the man you are now."

He knew this was when he needed to let her go, but instead Piper sat back and didn't resist when he curled her against his side. She laid her head on his shoulder and he just sat there enjoying feeling each breath she took.

"Let's get you to bed, baby. It's been a hella day. I'll take the truck."

"No, it's your trailer. And you have to compete tomorrow. I'll take the truck. Or sleep here."

His heart lurched in fear at the thought of Piper alone in a field full of cowboys and ranch hands.

"Not going to argue about that. No way would I let you sleep in the truck without me when there will be dozens of half-drunk cowboys and stock hands around. You get the trailer."

"You could go to your parents' ranch."

He kissed her forehead. "Not leaving you on your own, Piper." His heart felt heavier with each attempt she made to think of his comfort instead of hers. "We'll sort the rest out tomorrow after the short rounds."

Piper huddled under a beautiful plaid wool Pendleton blanket she and Boone had bought on a trip to Portland, Oregon, in August. She watched Boone, freshly showered, and in a sweatshirt and sweats, walk toward her with a steaming, fragrant cup of tea.

"Ginger spice, your favorite," he said.

Piper fought back the spurt of tears and took the tea. Her hand shook. She sipped it as she watched him over the rim. Boone looked uncomfortable, restless, and her heart broke even more.

She found herself waffling. Was it so dumb to want one more night? To be held and to savor it because it would be the last? A gift to him and a gift to her. A night where she could remember every detail of the way he felt when he was in her arms. The heat of his skin. The way he always paused and looked into her eyes and whispered her name before he joined their bodies.

"I'll head outside, now," Boone said quietly.

Piper felt her heart jump, and lurch into her throat, suffocating her. She stared at the yellow stripe in the blanket, her mind suddenly awash with panic as her heart thundered in her ears and closed off her throat. She couldn't breathe. She couldn't think. Pinpricks of light burst behind her eyes.

"Piper." Boone took the tea from her hand as it started to slosh out.

"Baby, what's wrong?"

She bent her head down as agony and embarrassment swept through her. She could hear her shallow breaths sawing in and out of her tight throat. This was so dumb. Panic because he was leaving. She'd lived through this part before so many times. She was used to it. Over it. Why were her childish panic attacks resurfacing now? She hadn't had one since she was fourteen, and her father had slapped her to snap her out of it.

But instead of curling up in her closet alone, Boone was there, holding a bag that had earlier contained some apples she'd bought at Monroe Groceries in town. He sat on the bed and held the bag over her mouth.

"It's okay, baby. I got you."

He pulled her onto his lap and his hold hand—the one that could keep him astride a bucking bronc or bull—was gentle on top of her head, stroking down her hair over and over.

It took Piper an embarrassingly long time to pull herself together.

She thrust away the bag and then grabbed it back, folding it precisely like it was origami.

"Sorry." She squeezed her eyes shut. "I'm fine now."

So embarrassing. God, he was going to be so glad to get out of here, get away. The inconvenient ex-girlfriend who clung and panicked and didn't have a clue how to end a casual fling properly.

"Sorry," she said again.

"Baby," he said so tenderly. "Feel pretty shaky myself."

It was so Boone—kind, self-deprecating, trying to ease the tension—that she laughed even as tears started leaking out of her eyes.

She wanted him to stay so badly. Hold her. But that wasn't fair. It was over. She had to be mature about it. Let him go. Let him find himself. Be who he wanted to be even though she thought he was perfect now.

"Sorry. I'm okay now. Haven't had one of those in a while," she said, trying to sound brisk, while she scrubbed at her tears with the palm of her hand.

"You're sure?" He hadn't stopped holding her or stroking her head.

Boone would be a great dad, she thought in despair. He wouldn't close his child off in their room for crying or panicking or asking too many questions. Piper pressed her lips together so tightly they hurt. She had to pull herself together. And he had to get out of here for her to do it because he was one giant reminder of everything she wanted and couldn't have.

"I'm okay. I'm fine," she lied. "That was stupid."

"Piper, nothing you've ever done was stupid."

He sounded so admiring that it grounded her a little. "You'd be surprised." She tried to keep the bitterness out of her voice. "There's a long list."

"Doubt it. I'm pretty sure mine's longer. Here, let me check that you didn't burn your hand when the tea spilled."

He took her hand in his big, warm, calloused one, and Piper shivered.

"Does it hurt?" His voice was so gentle Piper almost wished her hand were burned just to see how he'd take care of her, just to have him hold her a little longer.

And that was wrong. Weak. She heard her father's voice again, always critical, scathing. But it had been worse when he'd been indifferent. Ignored her.

"No. It's fine. I'm fine. You should get some sleep."

"I will," he said softly. "You lie back down." He helped to ease her back into the bed and tucked the comforter and blanket up to her chin like she was an eight-year-old who'd had a bad dream.

His fingers gently stroked through her hair. "Close your eyes, Piper."

"But what about you?"

"I'll wait until you fall asleep, baby. Just relax, breathe. In. Out. I'll be right here until you sleep. Promise."

PIPER WOKE UP several hours later to an unfamiliar sound. It took her a moment to realize what the soft sound above and around her was—rain almost like a disembodied voice. She listened to the soft tapping on the roof of the trailer.

Was it a sign of renewal or of darker days ahead?

Piper had always loved the rain. Automatically she reached for Boone. His side of the bed was empty, cold;

comforter and blanket smooth. Piper sat up, agony and longing rushed through her. But more than that: practicality. Boone was outside in the rain, or cramped in his truck—not remotely ideal conditions for him to endure the night before a competition, though Boone would be the first to shrug it off. He was cowboy tough, always.

She needed to channel a little of that.

She quickly climbed out of bed and flung open the door and in her tank and small exercise shorts, she hurried out into the rain.

Figured tonight it would rain. Boone hopped up and quickly began rolling up his bedroll and sleeping bag. The rain was chilly and ran down his back like icy fingers all the way to the waist of his drawstring sweats.

This was only the beginning of how much this day would suck. His fault for sitting on the fence, for waiting for answers, for living in the moment.

He caught a flash of Piper, feet and legs bare as she jumped out of the trailer. He hopped out of the bed of the truck, stashed his bedroll in the back seat of his cab and then strode toward her, but she was already there, bringing him up short.

She shivered, her arms wrapped tightly around her body.

"Baby, let's get you back inside. You're soaked, and it's freezing out here."

The life-giving drizzle had briefly turned into a downpour.

"Baby, your feet." He shook his head, charmed, exasperated, and worried she'd step on broken glass or a stone that would hurt her. Cowboys were not always the most considerate of cleaners-up.

He knew it was wrong, but it felt so right to pick her up and carry her back to the trailer. One-handed he opened the door and fed her inside, not quite trusting himself to not follow. She'd felt fantastic in his arms, and he ached for her. Hadn't been able to sleep and the rain had been a welcome relief to get up and stop pretending to try.

"Okay, get dried off and get back in bed."

"What about you?" Piper threaded her fingers through his and held on tight.

Killing him. He had no resistance around her. None. If he had, he wouldn't have hurt her and gutted himself in the process.

"I'll be fine. I'll sleep in the truck. Done it lots of times."

Her eyes searched his, and Boone felt like he'd sliced himself open and she could see all of him—his doubt, his desire, his vague dreams he was unable to articulate when hers were spelled out and listed in neon, and he wanted her dreams checked off for her—fulfilled one by one. He wanted Piper happy.

And he wanted to hold her tightly, promise her he could be that man, and to know that he wasn't wrong, that he wouldn't fail her.

"You don't have to," Piper said.

"Piper. I've fucked it up and dug a deep enough hole this weekend. No need to keep digging." He tried to smile and failed.

"No, Boone, don't think like that," Piper said, and Boone marveled at how she was so quick to forgive. "Your feelings aren't wrong. They are just your feelings."

He wished like hell he knew what his 'feelings,' hell, his thoughts were. His emotions—such as they were—veered all over the place, making him feel a little crazy and a lot sick to his stomach.

"Piper," he croaked out hoarsely.

This was a bad idea. Very bad.

She tugged and Boone followed her inside the trailer.

Chapter Twelve

BOONE ROUNDED THE corner of the largest barn where the horses were housed. He had his bull rope over his shoulder and work gloves on as well as his rosin. It was just past dawn. He'd fed and brushed Sundance, and talked to him while he'd worked and mucked out his stall.

He checked his phone. He had an hour before the pancake breakfast started. He knew Piper had a few early clients so once he finished he'd swing by her tent and wait until she finished. She'd scared the hell out of him last night with her panic attack. He couldn't stand to see her hurting. It gutted him.

Lying next to her last night, him on the outside of the comforter, her below, had brought him some measure of peace, although he'd had to fight the urge to pull her tight in to his body. He hadn't thought he'd be able to sleep, but when he'd woken shortly before dawn, Piper had been tangled around him, her hair a shroud, and like a dumb, weak bastard, he'd let himself soak her in for a few breaths before he slipped from the bed and left for the day.

He'd left her a note that there was a pancake breakfast in the park and that he'd stop by to see if she wanted to go. He also told her that they could talk after the rodeo, that she could use the trailer as long as she needed, that he'd drive her or take her anywhere she wanted to go.

All the right things.

But everything about his life today felt wrong. Wrong. Wrong.

He settled against the outside wall so he could feel the rising sun on his face, while he rosined his bull rope as well as his grip for Sundance. He watched the hands of the few stock contractors come and go—chatting in Spanish and English, flipping each other shit and teasing about what had or hadn't gone down last night at the steak dinner.

Boone briefly closed his eyes, desperate for the familiar calm to settle over him, to once again feel pleasure in the small aspects of rodeo life. Today he felt stiff, awkward, out of rhythm when usually he loved the work. The cowboys. The simple tasks. The focus. Sundance. Only usually Piper sat with him and talked to him while he worked his ropes. Or she'd read quietly, her feet tangled with his. He tested his rope, rubbing his glove over it again and again, feeling the stickiness.

He came to his feet. He still had a lot to do, but he had plenty of time. He knew his parents were coming to watch his events today as well as his sister Riley, her band and his brother Witt, sister-in-law Miranda and their adopted daughter Petal.

No pressure.

Usually he thrived on pressure. Loved the edge in his gut. The buzz in his blood. But now he wanted to be done. Far away.

He'd let Piper down.

He was letting his family down. They tried not to say anything, but he knew his dad wanted him home to help with the ranch and the expansion into bull breeding and later stock contracting with the Wilders. His mom wanted him to stop risking his life and health with the rodeo, but she also wanted him to ease the burden on his father.

What did he want, Piper had asked?

No one had ever asked him that, he'd later realized, and now when he asked himself that same question, he didn't have the answer.

He wanted to feel like he'd accomplished something.

He wanted to be the kind of man he was proud of.

He wanted to feel like Piper wouldn't be settling if she stayed with him.

And just those three answers alone proved that he was doing the right thing moving on and letting Piper find her own path.

Boone watched a few cowboys showing some young kids lariat tricks. The kids were up early and waiting for their parents after spending the night at the rodeo youth campout last night. He loved that about the rodeo. The kids. The families. The fans. Giving back to the community. And then the challenge. The adrenaline when he dropped down on the back of a pissed-off animal.

Nothing like it. Ever.

Except spending time with Piper.

Boone finished his work. Even joined a small knot of young boys and talked with them about their campfire stories last night. He laughed when they tried to scare him with a local ghost story and then he ambled off, trying to inject more confidence in his walk as he approached his trailer. But he wasn't sure of his reception. Would Piper want to talk to him? Was he doing the right thing by continually checking on her? Treating the day like it was a little bit normal?

But he didn't feel right leaving her alone.

She must feel stranded.

He wanted her to know that she wasn't. He had her back. But what he wanted to do was tell her that he wished he were different, a better man. No, what he really wanted was to say 'fuck it. Let's stay together because the thought of not seeing you smile at me first thing in the morning and last thing at night makes me feel so empty inside I want to howl like a Yellowstone wolf.'

Mixed messages.

Brilliant.

He needed his head examined.

Needed the type of clarity that came from top-shelf

whiskey except that it really didn't.

No, better yet, he needed his ass kicked.

Piper wasn't in the trailer, but it looked really clean. Spare. He tried to stuff down the dread. He took a step toward the small closet, but stopped, his hand on the handle.

He was not ready for that shitty reality. He knew that much.

Boone left the trailer and headed to her massage tent. He tried not to change his expression, but knew he failed that test too, when he saw Dean Maynard exiting Piper's massage tent pulling on his T-shirt way too slowly for Boone's peace of mind.

He wanted to kick himself. After he kicked Maynard. They'd talked about this. How it was her profession. And he got that. He'd been remarkably level-headed even when a lot of the cowboys had razzed him about his girl putting her hands on so many other men.

Usually they kept their clothes on. Figured Maynard would push it.

Maynard jerked his head in greeting. Boone waited for the caustic, sexual remark.

"Thanks, Piper," Dean said. "I have way more rotation now."

Piper emerged from her tent, methodically wiping her hands on a scent-free wipe. Her white cotton coat was wrapped tightly around her slim body.

"That's good, Dean, but still you should ice it for fifteen

minutes two to three times within the next hour or so, and drink lots of water today—not whiskey."

"Yes, ma'am." Piper handed him his Stetson. He pushed it on and then touched the brim in her direction. "Good to know you, Piper. You take care now."

"Thanks." She smiled. "Hey, Boone." Her voice softened, and usually he liked that except it wasn't warm. It was tentative, and he hated that. "Everything ready for your big day?"

He shrugged. In truth he didn't feel ready for any of today. Not one fucking thing. Too damn bad. It was going to hit with the force of an IED anyway.

"I'm good." He resisted touching her. "Feel like a pancake? Fundraiser at the park."

She looked at her watch. "No thank you. I'm meeting someone at nine."

"Oh." Boone rocked back on his heels. "Who?" Fuck, he had no business asking that. "I mean where? I can walk you there or do you need a lift?" That sounded slightly less needy.

Piper hesitated, and he felt a frisson of nerves crawl down his spine.

"Okay," Piper said.

He held out his hand. She hesitated.

"Sorry." He jammed his hands in his pockets.

He wore Wranglers today. He'd already caught shit from his dad about the switch to Levi's. Piper liked them. But now

Piper wouldn't give a shit about what he wore, and it seemed like a physical reminder that they were no longer a 'they,' only his dumb brain couldn't seem to get the message. And his body felt like six levels of hell.

He paused at the top of the bridge into Crawford Park and dug into his pocket.

He handed her a dime. "Close your eyes and make a wish."

Again, her eyes searched his. He felt like he was swimming in all that green. His dad used to take him and his brother and sister fishing in alpine lakes when he was young, and Piper's eyes reminded him of the lake shallows on a sunny day—green, sparkling, inviting and just a little touch of the mysterious.

"Why do you only have a nickel?"

"Your wishes are more valuable than mine," he said glibly.

"Don't say that, Boone." Piper's voice was fierce. "Don't even think it. That is so far from the truth. You are an amazing man. Amazing. And you'll find your way. I know you will."

Boone stared at her a little dazed by her passion.

"Let's wish together," he offered, needing the connection to her more than he ever had.

Boone palmed her fist holding her coin, his nickel pressed against the back of her hand, the bridge at their backs.

"Ready, set, go," he said and they swung their arms up together and the silver glittered in an arc, catching the morning sun—air shiny clear after the rain—before splashing down in the slow-moving creek.

And somehow, feeling Piper's hand in his, seeing the silver glint fly in the morning air, he felt the first stirrings of promise. Nothing had ever felt so right in his life as Piper. Nothing. And he had to find a way to hold on to that promise, find a way to deserve her so they could build the life she wanted with him in it instead of him floundering far away.

PIPER WISHED SHE didn't have doubts as she cupped her steaming chai and sat down at the table where Amanda waited, her blonde hair shiny and silky as it tumbled down her back. She wanted to feel excited. She wanted to feel sure. She didn't want to feel so hollow inside.

She felt like she and Boone could still have a chance, but she had to be true to herself. And maybe some time apart would give him some clarity. It was a risk. She knew that. But one she felt she needed to take. She was worth it. Boone was worth it.

"Hi, Amanda," Piper said approaching the table.

Amanda stood up and gave her a warm hug.

"It's good to see you. Thanks for meeting me and taking a chance on me renting the room in your salon."

"I think it's going to be a great match," Amanda said looking at Piper appraisingly. There was kindness and a touch of sympathy. "I wasn't actively looking to rent it out. I felt the right person would find me and the salon, but when we met and spoke I just had a really good feeling."

Piper saw Boone standing outside the Java Café still, an indecisive look marring his handsome features. She felt torn. She wanted to run to him, even as she knew she needed to walk away.

"You know Boone usually comes home a lot during the rodeo season. And he spends his tour breaks on the ranch." Amanda clearly noticed Piper was distracted and staring out the front window. "If you're hoping to avoid him, Marietta isn't the best place to settle. But if you're hoping that he'll come home for good for you, that plan has a chance."

The words filled her with hope and despair.

"I don't really have a plan on that front," Piper said with dignity. "Boone has to find his own path, and I need to find mine."

"Are you certain, Piper, that you're ready to strike out on your own? That you're ready to take this risk and settle in Marietta even with Boone still touring?"

"I know it seems like I'm taking a calculated risk." Piper dragged her attention back to Amanda. "And I'm probably in big fat denial if I say that I don't hope he'll want to continue to be with me, but…" She paused as she saw Tucker and Tanner enter the café and go to the counter to order what looked like a lot of coffees since Tanner grabbed three to-go carriers, and Tucker was already reading orders off her phone while her sister helped to write the orders on the side of the cup. Tucker looked up, spotted her and grinned, and gave her a thumbs-up.

"Stay put! Let me get these orders in."

Piper felt warmth bloom in her chest. Shane had offered her studio apartment to sublet for three months until the lease was up; Amanda had a room in her salon where she could set up her business. She had enough savings to survive while she built up her clientele. Miranda had offered her doctor husband up to introduce her to the physical therapy team at the hospital and she had a few budding friendships. Yeah, it would take work, but building her future was worth the effort.

"I'm certain," she said.

Piper walked back along Main Street. The rodeo was about to start, but she lingered at the stands of the few remaining sidewalk vendors. She really should be saving her money, but it was tempting to get a present for Boone—something that he could remember their time together by. Piper wasn't confident that she'd find anything that could possibly signify how special he was to her until she found a collection of beaded wrap bracelets for women and some thicker leather bracelets for men.

She eyed a black braided bracelet. It had a few copper beads threaded through the design as well as some other beads that were pale blue and reminded her of sea glass—where they met, in California. The bracelet was hooked over a Montana quarter. She eyed the animal skull.

The design was stark, powerful and a little edgy. Artistic but screamingly masculine.

Perfect.

Piper paid and tucked the box with the copper-colored bow into her backpack.

BOONE HAD BEEN worried that his head wouldn't be completely in the game, but he felt the familiar calm settle over him as he waited to be called for his first event. He'd managed to shove his entire life aside as he shrugged into his protective vest and went through his pre-ride ritual while he waited for his name to be called for the bucking bronc. He ran his rope through his glove back and forth five times. Stomped his left foot twice then his right twice. He squatted down. Breathed in deep and then out. And popped to his feet. He stretched out his arms.

And when his name was called, he hopped up on top of the chute and watched the back of the restless bronc shift side to side aggressively.

"Hell, yes."

He'd royally fucked up with Piper, but this, this he was

going to slay.

Boone ran his boot along the back of the bronc, making it stir even more uneasily. Murmurs ran round the chute staff, and Boone felt his pulse kick up.

Beautiful.

He dropped down on the bronc and immediately began to adjust his hand pull. He could feel the power of the animal beneath him and his body easily adjusted while he got his balance and hold set.

He needed this ride.

He nodded his head; slide of metal and it was on.

It was an epic ride, and Boone jumped off with more determination than he'd had when he'd climbed on. He was a cowboy, and he had come to win.

He was still in the zone when his dad joined him by the chute for his second event: steer wrestling.

"Going to beat your time from yesterday?"

"Likely never," Boone said, keeping his mind on visualizing the next ride, dropping down on the steer as soon as it cleared the chute. He wanted to focus on the steer rather than on the fact that after his bronc ride, he'd scanned the grandstands hoping to catch sight of Piper even though he'd told himself not to look.

But there'd been no sign of her.

That was for the best, he told himself. Still didn't believe it.

"Hella ride on the bronc earlier," his dad said.

Boone didn't count his scores or wins or money until the competition finished so he let the compliment roll off him.

When he was called and he'd settled on Sundance, he felt like a machine. He nodded his head, and as he burst out of the chute, he threw himself onto the steer, grabbed, twisted, rolled, held and then released as he popped up. It was over almost before he realized he'd started, although he had hit the dirt hard.

That was going to hurt tomorrow.

Like everything else in his life.

"Damn." His father laughed. "Freaky fast. I never once did it under 3.4."

A 3.3. Boone shook his head, feeling good. Last year's disaster was finally in his rearview mirror. One more event, the big daddy bull riding. His favorite.

"I'm going to meet up with your mother for lunch," his dad said quietly. "Join us?"

Boone's gut tightened. "Nah. Got some things to do."

His father looked him in the eye. "Can I count on you to come to the ranch this week?"

"Not sure. Made a promise. Not sure how it will play out yet."

His dad took off his Stetson, ran his hand through his hair and then reset his hat back on his head. Boone felt like he'd seen a ghost. He did that exact same thing when he wanted to say something, but wasn't quite sure what to say or how it would be received.

"Just spit it out," Boone said. "But I made a commitment." His time wasn't his own this week because he didn't know where Piper wanted to go.

"That's just it, Boone, you didn't make a commitment to anyone, not even yourself, and I think that's what's bothering you the most."

What the hell? Was his dad trying to be freakin' Yoda? "There is no try, there is only do," Boone loosely quoted what he remembered from a *Star Wars* movie. Well, George Lucas got that about right. And Boone intended to do so as well.

As if to prove a point to himself, after he stabled Sundance, Boone scrolled through his phone looking through the Paradise Valley land auction site. He'd done this often over the years, dreaming. Maybe it was time to make the jump. Figure out what he'd do with a chunk of land later, or more honestly, figure out how he'd do what he'd thought about doing since he'd been a teenager helping his dad work with kids in rodeo schools and 4-H clubs and FFA.

He paused on one parcel of land. It was finally going up for auction in October. Excitement and nerves flared. Normally he wouldn't consider it. He wasn't ready. Wasn't sure he had the funds saved for the down payment. But he couldn't keep living his life that way—putting every decision off, never making a plan. He took risks every weekend on the tour, but he trained. Maybe now it was time to take a different type of risk.

Deep in thought, Boone walked toward Piper's tent. Only it wasn't there. He did a double take and then wound his way slowly through the maze of trucks and trailers. The field was still full with the rigs of rodeo participants and support staff, but more than a few cowboys who hadn't made the cut to the short round had pulled out last night or early this morning to return to families or jobs. He looked in the back of his truck. Nothing. He blinked as if the rolled blue vinyl and tent poles would magically appear.

Boone bounded up the trailer stairs and went inside. No Piper. Also he realized why it was so clean and empty-feeling. Piper's large flowery duffel bag on wheels was gone along with the toiletries she'd had stashed in a blue and white striped canvas tote. He stood in the middle of the small space. Nothing of Piper remained. Just memories and a whisper of her scent.

He slowly sat on the bed. Stared at the carpet. He'd chosen it, cut it, laid it, paid for it when he and his dad had bought the trailer used from a retiring bronc stock coordinator.

"Boone?" He looked up feeling a little dazed, almost thinking he'd imagined Piper's voice.

"Hey." She stood in front of him.

"Where's your stuff?" he asked. "I told you I'd help you pack it up and take you wherever you wanted to go."

Piper's fingers brushed along his hand before she put her hands down by her sides. Her beautiful fiery red-blonde hair was pulled back in a sleek, low bun, but she wore jeans and a tank top and the western-style snap shirt she'd bought her first day in Marietta.

She looked beautiful and sad.

"I know. No need."

"Piper, I'm not just going to leave you to…"

"I know." She covered his hands with hers. "I've…um…decided to stay." Her eyes were steady.

"Where?"

"I'm going to stay in Marietta."

"Marietta?"

Piper took a deep breath. "I know I probably seem like a stalker, but of all the towns we've been to, I like this one the best."

"Piper, you can't just randomly start up a new life in a town you've only been in a few days," he said. "I will only be here during the off-season and…"

"Boone, this has nothing to do with you," she interrupted firmly. "I know it looks like I'm staying because this is your town, but really the plan was always for you to show me the west, and you did. You took me to small towns all over Montana, and Utah, and Colorado. We even went to a few places in New Mexico and Wyoming. I've seen it. I went to school in Southern California, and that was too hectic, too big, too anonymous for me."

She was staying. Piper would be in Marietta. Part of him rejoiced, but another part didn't know how to feel. He'd be too tempted to see her. And what if he came back from the last few rodeos and she was dating someone?

Fuck.

He shifted uncomfortably.

"But you've only seen Montana in the summer. It's cold in the winter, Piper. After Christmas the tourists leave except for a few avid outdoor sports fans. It's dark. Storms hit and the snow piles up."

"I'm sure I'll learn all about it, Boone," Piper said. "But this is my decision. I've lived a lot of places. I'm good at moving. Now I intend to get good at staying."

He stood up. "Piper, I won't lie and say I don't think about trying to win you back when I feel like I have more to offer you than a rodeo cowboy trying to make a name for himself."

"Love's not a game, Boone. I'm not a prize."

"You're everything I ever wanted in a woman, Piper."

"Boone, don't say those things. Aim higher in your ambition. You bring so much to the party. Don't count yourself so cheap."

"Yes, ma'am." He made her smile. "But what will you do? Where will you live?"

"I've rented a space in The Wright Salon to do massage. I found a furnished studio to sublet for a few months. It's Shane Knight's. She said she's going to travel a little and head home to Tennessee in a few days or a week."

"You've been busy." He was stunned that while he'd

been second-guessing his decision, Piper had been planning the life she'd always wanted.

"There's even a dance studio in town that I'm going to check into to see if maybe I can teach some adult dance classes or yoga or Pilates in the mornings or evenings."

It was so strange. He was happy for her. Proud of her. And yet he couldn't quite let her go so she could fly.

"What about us?" The words were out of his mouth before he knew he was going to speak. "I mean, can I still text you from the road? Can I stop in and say hi when I'm back at the ranch?" he asked even though he was the one who had decided he needed to end the relationship so Piper could move on and he could figure out what he wanted for a future.

"Not right away," Piper said. "I think we need time apart. I know I do so that I won't hope that you'll want to…you know." She sucked in a shaky breath and stared at the floor. "Get back together," she mumbled.

What was life without hope? Boone rejected that conclusion.

"You go your way. I go mine," she said in a low hollow voice that hit him like a mallet, hard in his gut.

"That sounds so final."

Piper nodded. She swallowed hard and then reached into her leather backpack and pulled out a small box with a ribbon around it. "I got this for you at one of the artist stalls. It reminded me of how we met, how we traveled, and how we parted. Take care, Boone." She pushed the box at him and then turned and left the trailer.

Boone held the box for a long time before he found the nerve to open it. Of course it was perfect. Trust Piper to find the gift that symbolized so much. Boone wrapped the leather around his wrist and fastened the Montana coin snap. He touched the copper beads and the transparent blue-green glass beads. He smiled.

Piper thought it was a goodbye gift, but why get him something that connected them, that he'd wear like a shackle and would see daily if she really meant goodbye forever?

Feeling a little more certain he was on the right path, Boone went back to prepare for his last event.

Chapter Thirteen

TWO WEEKS LATER Boone waled on what was probably his thirtieth fence post of the morning, while the still-pinkish morning sun slowly crept up into the sky. Two of the ranch hands were out repairing the south back fence line with him. The morning was chilly, but Boone was stripped down to his T-shirt and jeans.

Hitting so hard, working so fast was helping him not to think because he'd been doing too much of that the past couple weeks. What did he need to bring to the table before feeling like he could be a full partner at the ranch? What did he need to offer Piper to feel that he would make her a good life partner? Would buying his own small parcel of land make him feel deserving of the life his parents and their ranch offered? Was he ready to settle down, give up the rodeo and come back to the ranch full time, ask Piper to marry him? Would she even want to now?

So many questions and not an answer in sight.

His dad rode out in the truck. Boone had taken a horse, not wanting to wait for the crew or supplies and needing the freedom of a fast, chilly gallop.

Boone ignored him initially even when he saw that his mom had made a large thermos of coffee and snacks for his dad to bring. He'd been repairing and building fences since he was ten. He didn't need any help or advice.

He noticed the two hands had joined his dad and were chatting.

Fucking cozy. He had things to do. He continued to work, loving the way his muscles already ached.

Piper would be back from her morning run by now. Stretching out and doing some weight work. Or maybe about to hit the shower. He wondered if she had a client scheduled today. If she was lonely. If she missed him.

"You ever going to talk about it?" His dad stood beside him holding out a cup of coffee. Boone slammed down the fence post driver three more times, feeling the sink of the stake into the hard earth. This part of the ranch was as rocky as the moon. Exactly what he needed today because he was running out of time. He had to make some decisions. Take action. Prove to Piper that…

"Just trying to get caught up."

Hell no he was not going to talk about his feelings with his dad. Piper, yes, if she'd answer a text.

Boone, I love you as you are. He kept remembering Piper's declaration. The ring of truth in her voice. The intensity in her expression. But how could that be? He hadn't achieved much of anything yet. Nothing like his father had. He was just him. That's all he had to give her—himself.

"Coffee?"

"Busy."

"Take a break. Your mom also made breakfast sandwiches since you've been going without."

"I'm fine."

Boone loved the repetitive manual labor. It calmed his mind. But when he went to jerk out the old, bent and rusted stake to replace it, his dad put a hand on his shoulder. Boone fought the urge to shake it off.

"Drink the coffee. Eat the sandwich. Take a break."

Boone took the steaming traveler's mug. Held the sandwich. Wasn't hungry. He felt too on fire to eat. He looked around for a flat surface to put them down on.

"Drink. Eat," his dad repeated.

What the fuck? Was this some parental intervention? He was fine. Fucking miserable and no closer to figuring out what he needed to do to deserve Piper and his place at his family's ranch. But fine.

"I'll get to it."

"Now's good." His dad had his own cup of coffee. He took a sip and looked across the land. "You still have Copper Springs before the break and finals."

He knew his schedule.

"You're losing weight."

Boone shrugged. "Not a big deal."

"Is when losing strength can get you killed."

Boone unwrapped his sandwich. Took a bite. Tasted like dirt to him. He missed the ones Piper made with all the weird ingredients, some of which he'd never heard of. The thought of the egg and cheese and bacon would make her eyes roll back in her head in horror.

And then he would laugh. Threaten to kiss her with cholesterol on his breath. Or smear grease on her lips.

Then she'd push him away, laugh at him and run, and he'd chase and catch and then they'd…

Boone chewed and could barely get himself to swallow.

"Not really hungry," he mumbled.

His dad nodded. "So which part should we not talk about first?"

"Funny. Not talking about Piper."

"Good to know her name."

"Sure Miranda and half the town told you by now."

"Miranda told me she's still here. She's a masseuse. Witt said she's starting to get a few PT clients at the hospital clinic for therapeutic massage."

Of course Piper would succeed. She was smart, hardworking and awesome. And not just because he loved her.

He staggered a little at the L word. But it hit like a load of dumped fence posts. He'd avoided admitting that he loved Piper because they were supposed to be temporary. But he'd fallen hard and fast a long, long time ago. Million reasons. The way she looked at him like he was a hero always made him feel like one. The way she held him at night—

wrapped around him like he was her world. He loved to make her eyes light up, make her laugh, show her something new, make her feel safe and treasured. He loved that she was so curious about people and history and, hell, everything. He loved her kindness. Her sweetness. The way she took care of him.

Boone could barely breathe.

He'd thrown her love and care away.

Wanted her back with a fierce ache that clawed at his bones.

Needed her back.

He was barely existing, while she seemed to be settling into the town. She and Miranda had gone to a movie with Petal. She'd been shooting pool with Shane at Grey's one night, just before Shane left town. He'd walked in and walked out, trying to adhere to her no-contact rule although it was damn near killing him.

"It's too soon," she'd reminded him after the first late-night text when he'd been on the road, lonely as hell and wondering what he was doing without her.

In his mind, it was too long without contact so he'd resorted to often keeping his phone off so he wouldn't be tempted.

He couldn't eat or sleep. He just kept his eye on his goal. Winning the rest of the season. Accumulating more money. Going to that auction and getting that chunk of land. He thought he had a real shot. It was small and bordered by much bigger family-owned ranches. A little piece of it even touched his family's ranch. He had an idea about what he'd do with some of it. Not fully fleshed out. But he was in the process of being a better man, an independent man.

"Not in the habit of gossip at the pharmacy with Carol Bingley," his dad said sipping his coffee. "So Piper. What went wrong?"

"Seriously, I am not discussing my love life with you."

"So you love her."

Fuck. Boone jammed a huge bite in his mouth. Good delay tactic, but now he'd have to swallow.

Boone spit out the sandwich. "Why do you have to be so literal? It's a common phrase."

"Not for you. Not ever. And you won't look me in the eye. You've stopped talking. You don't joke with the ranch hands anymore. Work yourself harder than three men and have been competing like the devil's on your ass. So yeah, love. And you may not want to talk about it, but your mother's worried sick, and I don't like her to be upset. She has enough worry with Rohan out on another mission he can't talk about."

"Fine. I met Piper in California when I went to the stock contractor in Temecula to check out their operation."

"That long ago?"

Boone felt itchy. "Let's just drop it."

"Fine. What went wrong?"

"Nothing."

Everything.

"So she dumped you. Why?"

"She didn't dump me." Boone's pride was stung, and by the way his father took a sip of his coffee, his features carefully blank, Boone realized he'd been had.

"I'm just not ready to settle down," Boone said irritably, tired of trying to explain himself. "I need to achieve more. Be a better man."

"She say that?" His father's features tensed along with his voice.

"No, of course not," Boone defended Piper. "She said she loved me. That she couldn't imagine a better man for her. That she loved me as I am."

His father stared at him, his face as uncomprehending as Piper's had been. Why didn't anyone get it? Get him?

"It's just so goddamn easy for you," Boone burst out. "All of this is yours. You built it. You worked it. All of it is your achievement, and I'm just walking in. None of it's mine except by birthright."

"Bullshit," his dad said. "That's bullshit, Boone. It's not my ranch. It was my father's and his brother's. His father's before. And before that my great-grandmother inherited the ranch and ran it. It's not Taryn Telford Ranch. It's the Telford Family Ranch. Family. Father to son or daughter."

"You saved it."

"Hell yeah, risked my ass every weekend to save it. Bust it each day to work it. Keep it. For us. All of us. For you and

Witt and Rohan and Riley if they want. And your children. You started working the ranch hard when you were in elementary school, Boone. Learning the skills. Helping when you could and every day you got stronger and smarter about how to do things. You're ranch through and through.

"You have a gift with the animals and with the equipment. You keep everything running. Hell sometimes I lose you for days when you go help a neighbor with their big equipment. The point is we all work together. You're not walking into anything. You are part of it as much as I am."

"I just feel like I should bring something of my own."

"You do." His father's voice echoed his disbelief. "You bring yourself. Your skills. Your knowledge. Your way of solving problems. Approaching things. Your dreams. I don't expect the ranch to be static when you come on board. I expect you to agitate to make changes."

Boone pushed back his hat and wiped his forehead with his forearm. "I just want to achieve something on my own."

"Outside of ranching?"

"No." Boone kicked dirt over the food he'd spit out but animals and insects would make quick work of it. "I've always been your son. You've been an amazing dad. I just want to add on to that legacy, be my own man."

His father was quiet for a while. Thinking.

"You are your own man, Boone. Your decisions are yours. Your actions shape your life. When I married your mom and brought her here to live, my dad and uncle were still alive and working the ranch with me. I quit the rodeo and got to work. Your mom and I talked about things. She worked with the horses, but she also improved on the garden. Then later added crops. I wanted to buy more property. We saved so we could. Now I want to go into bull breeding. Expand stock-contracting operations. Each generation adds a piece. Once you get here and your heart and head are here, you'll start making changes. We'll work together as a family for a while, and then you'll take over and work with your kids and your siblings if any of them want to come home and make a life here. That's how it works."

Boone was quiet. He was starting to get what his father was trying to tell him. But he still felt like he needed to offer more to Piper.

"I want to build a career here," Boone said. "I want to put my own stamp on it. But I feel like I'm just bringing me."

And his savings from his winnings over the past seven years.

"That's all a ranch needs. Dedication. Willingness to work and share ideas."

Boone jerked his head in a nod. The words and what they meant were starting to settle in his head. Sound right. His father was verbally making him a partner. He'd bring his own ideas and skills to the ranch. Make changes.

And there were definitely things he wanted to do differently. Already after spending the summer with Piper he wanted to move the ranch over to organic. Grass fed. Antibiotic and hormone-free beef.

He looked at his dad.

"Need to finish the fence. Heading out tomorrow."

"I know. That's the other reason I'm here to help. But, Boone, don't leave it too long."

"The fence?" He'd been working on in since yesterday and would be done with this section by late tonight if he humped it.

"No. Piper."

"Dad, she deserves…"

"Let her decide what she deserves. When I met your mother, she knocked me off my proverbial horse. She was beautiful, educated, from a large ranching family that was way more successful than mine, out by Missoula. Your mom was way out of my league. I didn't care. Had to have her."

Boone laughed a little. It had been the same with Piper.

"And I didn't have much to offer. Me. A dangerous profession. A family ranch that was nearing foreclosure. And a burning desire to keep it in the family and make it thrive again. Your mother put her stamp on the ranch as much as I did. We worked together.

"Like when Witt went after Miranda, he wanted to make a damned grand gesture, so he made an offer on that fifty acres I had been waiting on to come down in price. He stole it from under my nose just to impress Miranda and show her that he meant business and planned to stay and put down roots here. I told him he should have waited for Miranda's input. If she were going to become part of the family, part of the ranch, she should have a say in what happens."

Damn genetics was a bitch. Boone had been planning the same move.

"Man you are today will be different in five years," his dad said, picking up quite a few stakes and easily balancing them over his shoulder. "Time changes you. The ranch changes you. The woman you fall in love with changes you. Fatherhood changes you. It's a process, Boone, for you as a man, and you and your wife as a couple. Not a damn destination."

EARLY MONDAY MORNING Piper entered the fairly crowded Java Café and spotted Tucker cuddled up with her husband and a few others whom she recognized from the rodeo a couple of weeks ago. Miranda was at another table huddled up with a few of the moms from the elementary school—likely planning a fall festival party or something else family-oriented. Piper ignored the pang of her heart and instead smiled and waved. Two of the women were clients and had booked second massage appointments.

"You knew it would take time to settle in," she chided herself under her breath.

Things were going as well as could be expected. While in line at the counter, she scanned the menu of drinks as if she didn't already know what she wanted. She should be happy, she reminded herself again. She'd chosen a town. Was making her stand here. It was cute. People were nice. She was already making some inroads socially, and her business, while not thriving, was at least up and running. Boone's brother, an orthopedic surgeon, and one of his partners, Wyatt Gallagher, had already introduced her to the rehabilitation staff at the hospital, and she'd discussed her training, experience and training both in massage and kinesiology and dance. She'd already worked with two post-injury clients from one of the physical therapists.

She also was going to meet with the owner of a dance studio in town to see if they had any desire to offer barre classes or adult dance classes or anything she could do at night so she didn't have to sit alone and stare at the bare walls until she fell asleep.

So she wouldn't have to think about Boone.

The weeks apart had not eased her ache or emptiness. She still had trouble falling asleep without him curled around her. And when she startled awake at night in the small studio apartment she'd taken over from Shane who'd left town several days ago, increasing Piper's loneliness, she couldn't get back to sleep.

Instead she'd make herself some peppermint tea and sit on the stoop of the outside stairs leading up to her studio and stare down the quiet residential street and feel lonelier than she ever had.

Maybe she shouldn't have told Boone to stop texting. Maybe she should start responding to his Snapchats.

But each picture, each short text had made her heart leap with hope, and her brain hyper-analyze. And then she'd worry about when the texts would slow. Stop. And she had to stop hoping. She'd told him she hadn't chosen Marietta because of his ties there.

Liar.

She knew Boone had placed two firsts in the rodeo over the past weekend. He was on fire. He was fine. Leaving her behind had been the right decision for him to regain his focus.

And she had to get on board with that. She had an early morning appointment. That had to be a good sign, right?

Piper ordered her chai and walked down Main Street, head up, scanning the street, still not quite able to believe that she had found her town even if she didn't have her forever man. Even if she wasn't his forever woman. She sipped her chai, determined not to fall into despair.

This was the hard part. It would get easier. She turned down Church and stopped. Blinked. No. She was hallucinating. She'd been thinking about Boone—when did she ever stop?—and she'd conjured him.

He paced out in front of the salon, which was not open yet. Quick, fluid strides, and even a block away, her heart lurched in her chest and then galloped wildly. Her breath pumped in and out as if she'd been running.

He was here!

It was all she could do to not toss aside her chai and start running toward him. Tell him she'd been stupid. A town without him would never be her home.

"Take a breath," she cautioned herself.

Maybe he just wanted to check on her. Make sure she was okay. Boone was kind. Responsible. He'd always taken care of her when they'd been together. And he'd let her take care of him.

And she'd loved every wonderful minute of it.

She pressed her lips together to stop the trembling. She forced herself to walk instead of run. But oh it was hard. He looked so good. The dark denim clung to his butt and muscular thighs. His dark blue tee stretched across his broad shoulders and kissed his pecs and hugged his biceps. He wore a pale blue chambray shirt, open. And he was playing with his Stetson, worrying it through his hands as he paced. He jammed it back on his head.

As if he sensed her hungry perusal, he stopped mid-pace, spun on his heel and stared at her with an intensity she'd desperately missed.

Every cell in her body woke up.

"Don't run," Piper whispered, holding herself rigid. "Don't cry. Cowards cry." She remembered her father's voice coldly making that statement so many times until she'd gotten herself and her soft heart under control.

She clutched her chai cup so hard it buckled a little. She

gulped in a deep breath and took a step toward him. And another.

And then he was striding toward her. His long strong legs that could grip a thrashing bronc and bull and hang tight ate up the ground and spit it out.

"Piper."

He stopped in front of her. Pale under his tan. His hands reached out to touch her arms and she leaned in toward him, melting. He barely skimmed her arms before jamming his hands in his pockets.

"Boone."

"Is it…is it okay that I've come to see you?" His voice sounded strained.

She felt her heart clutch in her chest.

"I know you asked me to stop…texting, but I…I…Piper." He stared at her with an intensity she'd only seen in him when he'd been looking at a hundred percent bull he'd been going to ride later. "I made a mistake."

Her stomach dropped, leaving her feeling more than a little sick. Boone's life was going well. He'd made a good decision for himself and wanted to tell her that, and she had to suck it up and wish him well. It hit her then how much she had still hoped that he'd come back to her. Want her.

"I thought that I didn't deserve your love because I hadn't accomplished everything I needed to yet. I thought I didn't deserve my place on the ranch because I wasn't bringing something tangible, something larger than myself to it."

He tipped his hat back and leaned down to look closer into her eyes. Piper felt a hot spurt of tears as that move was so familiar.

"I missed you," he said. "I feel like an idiot about so much—so casually uprooting your life. Not knowing what a true partnership really was even though I had the best example in my parents. You taught me that too, Piper, but it took me so long to wrap my head around it. To understand it here." He lightly tapped on his chest.

Piper had no idea what to say. He looked so good. So real. So solid. And she felt like she was standing in quicksand.

"Am I too late, Piper?"

"Too late?" she repeated trying to keep herself from hoping.

He took off his hat again, ran his hands through his beautiful sandy hair that was springy under his fingers. He hadn't cut his hair. God, she wanted to touch him.

"To fix this. To fix us."

She lightly touched the tip of her tongue to her lips, still not wanting to hope.

"Why?"

His face closed down a little. "I deserve that."

"No. I'm not trying to be bitchy. I just…I don't know what's changed."

"Everything. Nothing. Me. I've changed. I'm changing. I

want to keep changing with you. I said I regretted casually uprooting your life, but only the way I did it, not that I did it. The four months we were on tour was the best time of my life. Everything felt right. All the doubts I tried to push aside growing up about my place in the world were silent. You felt like home, Piper. Not the ranch. You."

"Boone," she breathed out shakily because she'd felt the same with him from the beginning and so much rode on this moment.

"I regret that I didn't trust myself enough to hold on to you. I felt that I needed to be more, achieve more. I thought there was this place I had to stand tall in, and that place would signal to me that I'd arrived, but I had it all ass-backward. It's not a place. Funny." He laughed bitterly. "Growing up my dad was always the smartest person I knew. I admired him so much and wanted to be like him even as I resented him for setting the bar so damned high, but he was right. He told me my achievements were a process not an end game. One more point in his tally column."

"I'm glad," Piper whispered. She was happy Boone had a father he could admire and learn from. She knew all about the bar being set too high to ever clear. "Boone, it's really good to see you."

It was hard to see him though. Harder than she'd imagined. All she wanted to do was throw herself in his arms, accept what he would give her.

But she needed to be loved.

She needed to be a part of his life, a part of his family.

"But it's really hard for me to see you and not want…to…" She sucked in a breath. "Not want to be with you again, but I need more from you."

"I know. I can do that now," Boone said eagerly. "I can prove…"

"Boone, a relationship isn't a science project, and you've really caught me off guard and I have a client arriving soon so I can't… I need to get myself together first."

She clutched her chai like a lifeline.

The tension drained out of Boone like she'd pulled a plug.

"Piper, what I'm asking for is another chance with you. I won't fuck it up. I promise."

What was different? How had he changed? But she could tell that he had. He seemed more intense. Less carefree. More driven. She missed his smile. His dimples. The way his eyes would light up when he saw her, but this new brooding fire stole her breath and made her body liquefy—embarrassing since it was just past eight in the morning and they were on a public sidewalk.

"I just need a chance. Yes or no, and I should warn you that I don't think I can accept no and will do everything in my power to change your mind, and I don't give up easily. So yes or no?"

No-brainer. She should be terrified. But hadn't she built her life on reaching for things that looked out of reach?

"Boone," she searched his dear face. He looked so fierce and determined, and all her doubts and fears dissipated like morning mist. "Yes. But your timing sucks because I have a client arriving. Actually, they're late." She tried to cling to her professional side when all she wanted to do was ditch it, and drag Boone inside and get skin to skin so she could finally feel warm and utterly alive once again in his arms.

"Nope. Your client's right on time. And I booked out your day."

She stared at him. The receptionist Emily hadn't clued her in at all that the four appointments for today had been booked by the same person. Had she been in on it or had Boone been really creative? He did have a large family to call on for help.

"So this was a plan?" she asked, not realizing until she said it that she was teasing him a little. Hard to do when she still couldn't breathe properly. When she still wasn't sure what he was telling her.

"Step one in my win back Piper campaign."

"How many steps are there?"

"Not sure. It's a process. Probably will take the rest of my life."

STEP TWO INVOLVED his truck and a trip. No blindfold this time.

"I remember this place," Piper said softly. "We had a

picnic here."

Boone leaned back into an indentation in a large slab of granite. The hill was large enough to provide views of the valley, rolling hills and the mountain ranges that hemmed it all in. He took a chance and reached for her, his hands loose around her waist. Piper stiffened for a moment and then nestled against him. He winced.

"What?" She tried to pull away.

"Nothing." No that wasn't right—he wanted to have a close and honest relationship with Piper. "I fractured a couple of ribs at Copper Springs in the short round yesterday. Still won," he couldn't help the brag, but he wanted Piper to know that he was skilled and tenacious and would take care of her, even as she took care of him.

"Boone." She turned to look up at him.

"Not a big deal. Not the first time. Might be the last if I'm lucky at the finals in January, but I'm wrapped, and holding you feels amazing."

Piper settled back, only more gingerly.

"So what changed your mind?" she finally asked.

"I don't think I changed my mind, Piper. You were always the one for me. The minute I saw you I was all in, but had no idea what to do with how intense everything got so quickly so I did what I always did, just went with it. I deeply, deeply regret that I hurt you, but I can tell you that meeting you and spending the summer with you was the best thing that happened to me, and I hope that meeting me and spending the summer at least makes your top ten list."

Piper turned in his arms. Briefly her lashes swept down, and then she looked up. Her eyes glinted with humor.

"Top ten," she mused. "I'm not sure, Boone. I might have to think about that for a while. I have a really long list. Did you bring a picnic this time? A blanket?"

"Are you teasing me, Piper?" His voice edged with uncertainty.

"Definitely. But I am hungry. I haven't been able to eat much."

"Feeling pretty hungry myself. I was hoping to take you someplace for lunch if you'll let me and if you want to go, but I wanted to take you back here first."

"Why here?" Her fingers played in his hair, and the pleasure was so intense that he closed his eyes and nearly moaned. How he had missed her touch. Her laugh. Her play.

"It's my favorite view in the valley. I used to hike here. Drive my truck here when I was older and taking a break. It's coming up for auction. It's not big enough to ranch, but big enough for other things."

"Like what?" Piper asked leaning in to him and pressing a soft kiss against his jaw.

"You're not even looking at it," he breathed. Did that mean she didn't like it? Wasn't interested in buying land or being with him?

"Because I'm looking at you."

He noticed that she was careful not to put her weight against him because he'd told her about his ribs—which was why he hadn't wanted to tell her. But her lips whispering back and forth along his jaw were causing one hell of a reaction.

"Tell me about the land, Boone."

"Would if I could think. You know what happens when you touch me."

"Be strong. Focus."

Boone groaned as she kissed a line down his neck and licked across his collarbone. Who the hell knew that was an erogenous zone before Piper?

"I was thinking I could start a small foundation to help fund a program for teens who'd gotten in trouble with the law or were struggling in school or at risk in some way and teach them rodeo and animal husbandry skills, and the basics of repairing a motor or an engine. Lots of kids out there who didn't get a good role model in a father, and I got the best. It could be an after-school program, just a couple of hours each day so I could still put in a full day at the ranch, and I know so many cowboys who've retired from the tour who'd be willing to help one afternoon a week.

"Last time I was at Big Z's I talked to the owner, Paul, about his policy on donations and helping out non-profits at cost, and got some good answers. Colt Wilder has helped build a lot of barns and other construction projects so he'd probably help us build a small barn here. Wouldn't need to be big. And a corral. Some fencing for pasture."

"You've given this a lot of thought."

He nodded. "Over the past few years, yeah, but it always seemed out of reach and too soon for me to start thinking this way. I felt like I had to be able to do it all at once, but after a talk with my dad who helped me see how I was looking at my life ass backward, I realized I could start with just one piece. Like you did buying the massage chair. And then the tent, and a few weeks later, the massage table, then the Pilates whatever that I caught so much kinky grief from until a cowboy actually had the balls to try it." He shook his head. "Fun times."

"So the land first."

He nodded. "Got enough saved for a good down payment. And an approval from a bank to carry the mortgage if my bid goes through. What do you think? Would you live here with me eventually when we saved enough to build a house? We could live on the ranch before that. I can convert one of the cabins or bunkhouses into a home for us or would you rather be in town?" Boone asked, a little nervous about her answer because he couldn't imagine not living on the ranch unless it was here and with Piper.

"Depends on where you are."

"With you. Always with you."

"You said you could convert a bunkhouse or cabin," she said softly as her hands played over his chest. "Would you teach me so we could build our home together?"

He nodded, so overcome with emotion that he hid his face in her neck and pulled her in tight—fuck his ribs. He ignored them, and knew Piper could feel his tears wet against her. He hadn't cried since he was a kid, but somehow even that was okay with Piper.

"I think it's beautiful here," she finally said, her hands now soothed down his back. "You could also have recreational opportunities for the kids on weekends—backpacking, hiking, camping, fishing, snowshoeing. I heard it snows in Montana."

Clearly she was giving him time to recover, but Piper, being Piper, her amazing brain was already adding on to his plans, and Boone felt so grateful he wanted to fall on his knees and thank God and the universe and every blade of grass in Montana that Piper was willing to take another chance on him.

"That's only a rumor," he said. God she was as smart as she was beautiful and he was beyond lucky. "I was thinking that if you were willing, we could stop by the ranch to have lunch with my folks. Riley's back at college. Witt's working at the hospital, Miranda will be at her gift store and their daughter, Petal, will be in school, but we could eat with my mom and dad. It's just sandwiches and usually a soup in fall and winter, salad in spring and summer because everyone will be heading out to go back to work, but I want them to meet you. I want to show you the ranch. I want you to pick out the place where you want us to make our home. I've missed you, Piper. Missed everything about you. Please, please come home with me." He cupped her beloved face in his hands just to feel her warmth and soft skin.

"Stay with me. Build a life with me."

"I'd love that," she said quietly. She leaned forward to kiss him, but he stopped her.

"I love you," he said. "I think I loved you from the beginning. I know I loved you when we were swimming in the hot springs pool in Ouray, Colorado, late June, and we had to jump out during the thunderstorm and we were running for shelter and you were holding my hand and laughing and you shared your towel with me. You're special, Piper. So special, and I want to be your man. I want to make you happy."

"You already do, Boone. You always have." She sealed the moment with a kiss, a sweet one, that soon grew deeper, more passionate, more like a vow, and Boone felt his entire world went right again after so much had felt so wrong for the past three painful weeks.

He didn't have the ring yet. But he had an idea. He'd sketched it out, snapped a picture and emailed Sky Wilder. She'd sent him some sketches back asking for his opinion. This week he was going to buy the diamond and flank it with Montana sapphires and when the ring was finished he was going to do it right, how Piper deserved. Totally romantic. A room at the Graff, roses, champagne or if the auction went well, maybe they'd bundle up and come here. Look out over their future and he'd get down on one knee and ask the most important question of his life.

"For a man who claims to live in the moment, you seem to have been doing a lot of thinking," Piper said.

"Don't tell anyone. Gonna ruin my rep."

"Your secret's safe with me."

"So yes to meeting my parents?"

"You already had your answer."

"Yes to bidding on this land?"

"Give an inch you want a mile."

"I want a lot longer than that, Piper. I want to travel a lot of miles with you and each one will lead us, eventually, back here. What do you say?"

Piper slipped her hand in his. "Yes, cowboy, let's go home."

The End

The 79th Copper Mountain Rodeo

Book 1: *The Cowboy Meets His Match* by Sarah Mayberry

Book 2: *The Bull Rider's Return* by Joan Kilby

Book 3: *Cowboy Come Home* by Sinclair Jayne

Book 4: *The Cowboy's Last Rodeo* by Jeannie Watt

Book 5: *The Rodeo Cowboy's Baby* by Heidi Rice

Available now at your favorite online retailer!

About the Author

Sinclair Jayne has loved reading romance novels since she discovered Barbara Cartland historical romances when she was in sixth grade. By seventh grade, she was haunting the library shelves looking to fall in love over and over again with the heroes born from the imaginations of her favorite authors. After teaching writing classes and workshops to adults and teens for many years in Seattle and Portland, she returned to her first love of reading romances and became an editor for Tule Publishing last year.

Sinclair lives in Oregon's wine country where she and her family own a small vineyard of Pinot Noir and where she dreams of being able to write at a desk like Jane Austen instead of in parking lots waiting for her kids to finish one of their 12,000 extracurricular activities. …

Thank you for reading

Cowboy Come Home

If you enjoyed this book, you can find more from all our great authors at TulePublishing.com, or from your favorite online retailer.

Made in United States
North Haven, CT
16 March 2024